Wait a moment. The second man looked familiar. Messy brown hair. Freckles. Tall.

And then he glanced up as if he felt her gaze on him.

Her entire world ground to a halt. Blood hardened into ice in her veins. The noise and chaos around her disappeared as she found herself gazing back into the bluest of eyes, which widened in recognition.

Her heart seemed to stop beating. Her lungs tightened and refused to draw breath. Black seeped into the corners of her vision. Dizziness tipped her one way and then the other as she swayed on unsteady feet. Her limbs grew heavy. And the last thing she was aware of was a pair of strong arms catching her before her world turned dark.

Through Wylder Meadows

by

Sydney Winward

The Wylder West

Through Wylder Meadows

Cover Art by *Tina Lynn Stout*

The Wild Rose Press, Inc.
PO Box 708
Adams Basin, NY 14410-0708
Visit us at www.thewildrosepress.com

Publishing History
First Edition, 2022
Trade Paperback ISBN 978-1-5092-4346-4
Digital ISBN 978-1-5092-4347-1

The Wylder West
Published in the United States of America

Dedication

To Morgan—that one change made the book possible!

Prologue

New York, 1879

Sophia Meadows lightly touched each piano key, her eyes closed as a beautiful melody filled the drawing room. A rush of joy, calm, and peace washed over her as her heart poured out through her fingers onto the keys. A beautiful daydream followed her music, one where she found herself outside. Golden sunshine caressed her face. The soft, silky petals of white daisies stroked her skin. Tall, purple lupines brushed against her dress.

A strong, freckled hand reached out for her, and her fingers crawled across the instrument in response to her frantically beating heart. Samuel, her dear friend, gazed back at her with eyes bluer than summer skies, filled with more life than the vast seas.

He grasped her with sturdy hands, a smile lifting on his freckled face. His messy dark-brown hair swept across his forehead as he spun her in a dance. Their laughter filled the flower-filled meadow of her daydream, a melody of rapture and beautiful promises of the future.

They stopped dancing and gazed into each other's eyes. He caressed her cheek with rough fingers, and—

"Miss Sophia."

Her heart leaped out of her throat, her eyes

snapping open as her fingers pounded on the piano keys in her fright. Instead of a beautiful meadow, four walls surrounded her and jarred her from the daydream. Her pulse thrummed faster than a wild horse with hounds nipping at its heels.

She took a deep breath and smoothed her clammy hands over her skirt. Another moment passed before she raised her head to meet the butler's gaze as if she hadn't just been daydreaming about the man she had loved for years. The friend who was completely oblivious to her feelings. "Yes, Mr. Hopkins?"

The gleaming black wood of the Bechstein grand piano called out to her, whispering promises of beautiful, *uninterrupted* daydreams. But she kept her hands in her lap, despite how much they itched for ivory keys, laughter, and golden sunshine.

"A messenger is here to see you." He formally held his wrinkled hands behind his back. The man's thick, white mustache hid his upper lip as he cleared his throat. "I believe he has news of Mr. Samuel."

"Samuel." She gasped.

In a graceful yet completely unladylike movement, she slid from the piano bench and rushed out the door, down the hallway, and skidded to a halt when she spotted a man standing in the foyer.

He wore a vest over a loose brown shirt, a hat held to his chest, and a pair of brown leather gloves over his hands. Short facial hair covered his face, and he gazed back at her with serious brown eyes.

"Jason Smith, ma'am," he said with an incline of his head. "I'm Samuel Woods'…colleague."

The man held out a crumpled and dirtied envelope as if it had trekked miles just to arrive at her doorstep.

Eagerness to hear from Samuel tore at her carefully constructed facade, though she forced herself to take the envelope calmly. She ripped it open nonetheless.

" 'Dear Miss Meadows,' " she read. " 'I regret to inform you...' " Sophia trailed off, stones of dread piling up within her stomach as she read the words on the paper and then reread them. Her knees buckled beneath her, and she collapsed into a chair.

Samuel Woods' death...got trampled by a horse...funeral arrangements have already been made...

"No," she whispered, shaking her head as she finally lifted her gaze to find regret in Jason's eyes. "This isn't true. Samuel is careful with horses. He would never have let this happen."

Yet the words stared back at her on the page.

"It was dark. And muddy. I didn't see it happen myself. But the body..."

Her grip tightened on the letter, adding a few of her own crumples. This had to be a mistake. Samuel worked as a ranch hand in Pennsylvania. No one commanded a horse better than he did.

Again, she shook her head. Tears welled in her eyes until the man before her looked like a blob of brown. Beautiful memories flashed across her mind of her playing in the river with Samuel when their parents turned their backs. The laughter when they'd thrown mushy, rotten apples at each other before getting scolded for their soiled clothes and sour odor. The nights spent on the porch swing just talking and gazing at the stars.

His beautiful smile. It couldn't be gone forever.

Her hand trembled, rattling the letter. "I don't

believe you."

But then he reached into his pocket and pulled out a silver locket with flowers and swirled designs etched into the metal. Her lungs constricted, air refusing to enter as she stared and stared. Numbness crawled into her mind and settled into her heart. Her locket... The one she'd given to Samuel before he left for the job in Pennsylvania after his father died.

When she didn't reach out for the piece of jewelry, he placed it on the circular table beside the chair with a *thunk* of finality.

"You ought to know he treasured it. I think he would have wanted you to have it." He placed his hat back on his head and tipped it in farewell. "I'm sorry for your loss, ma'am."

Mr. Hopkins opened the door for him, and just like that, the man left the estate, leaving behind a heart wrought with open wounds.

Silence filled the foyer as she stared at the black-and-white checkered floors.

Samuel...

Samuel...

Samuel...

Each heartbeat echoed his name, bouncing off painful, bleeding walls. The world around her became blurry again. The words on the letter in her hands jumbled together. The black-and-white floors blended in a cloudy mass.

"Miss Sophia," the butler said softly. His voice snapped her out of her numb daze. A sob bubbled up in her throat, and then another. She snatched the locket from the table and wept as she ran past her concerned sisters' stares and up to her room. She slammed the door behind her, and when her grief expanded within her chest, she grabbed a pillow from her bed just in time for her scream to burst out of her and into the soft fabric.

The muffled scream was followed by another and another until her throat was raw. Her heart still bled. Her dizzy head pounded.

With relentless sobs, she grabbed the picture frame on her writing desk, one of Samuel standing beside a horse, wearing a hat and a gun in a holster on his belt. She smashed it onto the ground, glass flying in all directions.

"Why?" she shouted to Samuel, to the blasted horse, to God.

Too suddenly, her strength left her, and she collapsed to her knees. The bite of glass into her skin was nothing compared to her shattered heart.

She wiped her eyes and gazed at Samuel's handsome picture buried beneath a pile of glass shards. Carefully, she pulled out the photograph and gazed at the sepia image. Happiness filled his expression. He'd loved working with horses. How could something he cherished so much be the thing to take his life?

Her hands trembled as she dug into her desk for a pair of scissors, cutting his face out of the photograph in an oval shape. The locket's metal had gone cold, no warmth in its depths as she opened it. On one side of the locket was her face. She placed Samuel's image on the opposite side and snapped it closed.

When she hung the piece of jewelry around her neck, the weight nearly dragged her down into the darkest pits of grief. But if she kept him close to her heart, always, then he couldn't truly be gone.

Someone knocked on the door, and moments later, her father entered. Although he said nothing, his expression full of pain and sorrow spoke volumes. Not just for her own grief, but because Samuel had been like a son to him. Like family. He held his arms open, and she flew into the comfort of his embrace, weeping until no tears remained.

She clutched her locket in her hand. Samuel had been torn away from her so quickly. She hadn't even been able to say goodbye.

Chapter 1

Two years later

Samuel Woods licked his parched lips and arched his aching back from where he crouched in his horse's saddle. He dared to blink his dry eyes only twice before he resumed staring at the saloon from his position in a copse of trees. A dry, dirt road led to the establishment, a single lantern hanging beside the door a beacon to late-night patrons. A half-moon hung in the dark, September sky, offering the smallest bit of light as they waited.

And waited.

"Do you think he'll be in there all night?" Jason Smith asked beside him, making him jump.

"Gah!" His voice croaked from his dry throat. He shot the man a glare as he resisted reaching for his waterskin to save what he had left for the return journey. He rolled his tense shoulders and rubbed his burning eyes. "At least give me a warning before you talk and scare me like that."

"Sorry, Samuel." However, the man's grin was unrepentant.

"I asked you to call me Ellis, remember? What if someone overheard you calling me Samuel?"

"There ain't nobody out here except us. Unless you count the horses, but they keep secrets better than any animal I know. Loyal to a fault."

His colleague and friend patted his horse's neck before leaning forward and offering the animal an apple. The bored horse took the fruit greedily between its large teeth, and Samuel winced at the deafening crunch as it bit through the core and chewed.

Too loud. What was Jason thinking?

"Stop worrying so much." Jason rested his arms on the pommel of his saddle. "I've only slipped up once in two years."

"Yes. *Once*, giving your real name in front of the only person I wanted you to be careful around."

"Sorry, I panicked. She was pretty."

Samuel frowned as his thoughts turned to his childhood friend, Sophia Meadows. The guilt of his awful lie about his supposed death pressed heavy on his shoulders and even heavier when his mind drifted to the locket he'd forced himself to return. Cutting ties completely was the only way he knew to keep her safe. But it didn't stop him from thinking about her once in a while. Or perhaps more than once in a while.

Along with his back, his chest ached. Her friendship—as well as their mutual friend Amelie's— had been the only thing keeping him grounded. Now that he'd severed the roots, he had nothing to call home. Not anymore.

Jason sighed long and hard. "Some days, I really want a wife. You know. Settle down. Start a family. I'm thirty years old. Maybe it's time. What about you?"

"It's not happening."

Four years younger than his friend, he knew his work was dangerous. Too dangerous. Especially for a wife and children. What occupation could he possibly trade it for? He was good with horses. And guns. But that was about it.

"Keep focused." He nodded to the men staggering out of the saloon, drunk and with a couple of ladies on their arms. At this distance, their faces proved to be too difficult to make out.

Beside him, Jason rested his hand on the revolver at his waist. Shooting their targets was only used as a last resort, mostly in self-defense. And the bounty on this man's head was far too high to slip up and kill the man before delivering him. Alive.

One of the men leaned against a wooden post with his leg propped behind him, a cigar in his mouth. A flare of red burned bright in the darkness moments before smoke drifted in Samuel's direction on the slight breeze.

Four men in total. Two occupied with the women. One smoking. Another tending to the horses.

Four? Jason mouthed.

Samuel shook his head, never taking his eyes off them. Too many, but it wasn't something they hadn't done before. Unfortunately, the attempt had resulted in injuries and one man dead. He preferred they capture all of them alive.

The women said their goodbyes, and the four joined each other near the horses. It was now or never. If they didn't subdue McKinney and his gang now, tracking them to another city would prove to be difficult.

He eyed Jason, who nodded. And then he tipped his hat lower over his eyes, the signal.

A boy of twelve knocked over a barrel of water beside the horses and ran. The wooden barrel crashed to the ground and spilled its contents at their feet. The horses whinnied and reared in fright. Two of them took off at a gallop, their riders chasing after them.

"Come on," Samuel said, and they kicked their horses forward, hooves thundering on the dirt path. Beneath the moonlight's glow, he recognized the two remaining highwaymen as Cade McKinney and "Mute" Machk. McKinney drew his gun from his holster a second too late before Samuel jumped off his horse and tackled the man to the ground.

Fists flew in all directions. He punched McKinney in the jaw, only for him to return the favor to his gut. Dirt sprayed into the air, blinding and suffocating. McKinney delivered another punch to his gut and rolled him over, but before he lashed out again, a gunshot echoed in the skies.

McKinney leaped off him, and he and Machk mounted their horses faster than he thought possible. By the time Samuel climbed to his feet, the gang of four had disappeared from sight.

"No!" He kicked the dirt and then scowled at the passerby who held his gun into the air, the one who had fired the warning shot. "Do you realize what you've done? That was *Cade McKinney*." Or in other words, the man whose face was plastered on wanted posters all across the Wyoming Territory.

The man paled, visible even in the dim moonlight. He murmured an apology before scampering off with his tail between his legs.

Jason grunted behind him, and he turned to find his friend hunched over, his hands clutched over a bleeding wound in his shoulder.

He swore under his breath as he hurried toward his

saddlebags and dug inside. Several people watched, investigating the sound of the gunshot. "How bad is it?"

"A knife wound. I'll live."

When people continued to whisper and stare, he glared at them, and they quickly retreated. He hefted Jason to his feet and led him into the shadows of an alleyway before helping him to sit on a barrel against the side of a building. He borrowed the lantern hanging in front of the saloon to illuminate the alley. Blood soaked Jason's shirt, and when he eased the clothing off him, it continued to run in red tendrils down his arm.

"Why are you always the one getting stabbed?" Samuel asked as he threaded a needle and turned it in the lantern's fire until the tip glowed red.

"Why are you always the one gettin' shot?" Jason countered with a grunt.

"It was only twice. And one of those times, the bullet only grazed me."

Jason released a muffled cry when Samuel poured a flask of whiskey over his shoulder. He began stitching the wound, each stitch careful and unhurried. McKinney's gang was already gone, and he doubted Cheyenne's sheriff would investigate the gunshot, at least not yet.

Finally, he tied off the last stitch, wrapped Jason's shoulder in a bandage, and helped him into a spare shirt. How many times had they done this? He'd lost count.

A wry smile pulled on his lips. He supposed he possessed a few more skills other than horses and guns. He knew how to sew too. Mostly wounds. And buttons. Nothing more.

"We need to find out where they're headed." He

stared out in the direction the men had disappeared, and then his gaze moved toward the door of the saloon. "Do you want to take the lead, or shall I?"

With a roll of his eyes, Jason gave him a pointed look. "Wooing has always been your strong suit. You're wasting your talent on barmaids. I would find myself a wife if I were you."

"But you're not me."

Although Jason's movements were labored, they climbed the stairs of the saloon and entered. A bell tinkled overhead, and cigar smoke enveloped them in a cloud of haze.

At the late hour, most of the patrons had already left the establishment. Only a few stragglers remained. Two men sat at a table, each with a drink in his hands as they conversed, one of them blowing out smoke from their cigar. Another young man swept floors and cleaned tables.

Samuel's gaze drifted over their heads and landed on the tall blonde standing behind the bar. She busied herself with cleaning glasses and locking away whiskey bottles. Jason nodded his head in the direction of the woman, perspiration dotting his brow as he slumped into a chair nearest a window.

He needed to make this quick. Otherwise, they would lose precious time.

Confidence dripped from his swagger as he crossed the room. He leaned an elbow against the bar and angled his head to give him a better view from beneath the brim of his hat.

The woman across the counter paused as she dried a glass. Her mouth fell open as she stared back at him, and a small bit of color entered her cheeks.

He knew what she saw. It was what everyone noticed first about him and the one thing he wished he could change about his appearance. His eyes. A startling blue—something that made him memorable, easily recognizable, and he stood out like a sharp rock in his boot. His darned eyes made his job more difficult.

And sometimes easier as well.

He tipped his head and offered the woman a charming smile. "Ellis March. And what may I call the pretty lady across the counter?"

"Nuh-uh." The moment she fell out of her stupor, she wagged a finger at him. "I ain't spillin' for any bounty hunters."

With folded arms, he leaned even closer and layered on his charm. "What makes you think I'm a bounty hunter?"

"I see a lot of people come through those doors." She nodded her head in the direction of the entrance. "Sheriffs. Highwaymen. And you… You are somethin' in between a do-gooder and a lawbreaker."

Astute observation.

The woman would make a good spy. Perhaps if he wormed his way behind her walls of distrust, she could become a valuable asset to his assignments.

"Stop lookin' at me all determined like." Glasses clinked together as she placed them on the shelves against the wall before wiping a cloth over several beer spills on the counter. "Do you think you're the only man to make eyes at me? Gotta be tough as nails to work the bar, y'know."

"Fine." He took off his hat and placed it on the stool beside him while taking a seat. "Name your price."

"Ah, there you are." A grin made an appearance on her face moments before she ducked beneath the counter to continue her cleaning. "A serious fellow on the inside. An incorrigible flirt of a bounty hunter on the outside. I pity the woman who's tied you down."

"I don't have a woman." He frowned at the thought. His occupation took him all over the place. A woman deserved better than the life he could offer her.

The barmaid slapped the cloth on the bar, her hands on her hips. "I'll trade you information. For payment."

He placed a dollar on the bar between them. When she raised her eyebrows, he frowned and placed another down, which she snatched up. They'd better catch this guy. Otherwise, gaining information of his whereabouts would eventually drain his pockets.

"Cade McKinney." He glanced over his shoulder to make sure no one listened in. "Those men who just left. Where are they headed?"

"You didn't hear it from me." She also lowered her voice and leaned closer. "I caught bits and pieces of their conversation. More near the end when two were drunk. They're headed farther west to Wylder. And somethin' about a train, and about not getting caught in a smaller town."

"Train?"

She shrugged. "As I said, bits and pieces. They weren't talkin' about it for long." Her direct, brown eyes studied him for a moment. "What's your real name, Ellis?"

Quickly, he placed his hat on his head and tipped it in farewell. "Pleasure working with you."

"Lauren. Come back anytime." She grinned as she

fanned herself with the two dollar bills.

Not a chance.

His pockets wouldn't be able to handle the cost of her information. But this time, it was worth it.

He motioned for Jason to meet him outside, and only when they reached the horses did he dare speak. No sense in the blonde informant inside overhearing them. "McKinney is headed to Wylder. Something about a train."

"Wylder? I'm not sure I've heard of it." A wince contorted Jason's features as he pulled himself up into his saddle.

"The train passes through it. What do you think they're doing with the train? And why in Wylder rather than the station in Cheyenne? Besides, Wylder isn't too far from here. About fifteen miles." But far enough to make the journey difficult for his injured friend.

A frown formed on his face as he spotted a patch of blood on the bandage around his shoulder. "Jason, stay here and rest. You're in no shape to travel."

"So you can take the bounty for yourself?" Jason teased, but not without a grunt of effort. "I'm going."

"Fine. But if you keel over dead in the middle of the road, don't blame me." He swung his leg over the saddle, and with an excited whoop, he and Jason spurred their horses into action.

Dust kicked up around them. He lifted his bandana over his nose and mouth to keep himself from breathing it in. A life of excitement around every turn never failed to keep him interested.

Jason could have his wife and children and land. Samuel never wanted to give up his freedom.

Chapter 2

The train rocked back and forth, back and forth in a gentle, soothing rhythm. Filling the space of the window, sparse cabins and plentiful livestock stretched across wide amber fields. Green pastures, reflective lakes, and large mountains joined the unfamiliar scenery. Trees, sagebrush, and wooden fences dotted the landscape.

Sophia craned her neck when a herd of bison entered her line of vision. The bulky creatures grazed on green grass, one lifting its head as the train passed.

How much longer to California? Days had already passed with nothing to do but converse with other passengers and read the entire bookshelf she'd brought on the journey with her. A new, strange life awaited her in California. New people. New surroundings. A new fiancé.

She clutched her locket tight in her palm, an ache coursing from her fingers, up her arms, and through her chest.

When the ache festered and bled like an infected wound, she opened the locket and gazed at her and Samuel's photographs side by side. They made a great-looking pair. As if they belonged at each other's sides.

Her gaze traced his handsome features, every detail of him memorized. If only she could see the vast blue of his eyes one more time or hear his contagious laughter. If only he hadn't taken a piece of her heart with him to the grave. Even after the two years since his death, she still wasn't quite whole.

"You cannot wear another man around your neck after you are married." Her friend, Amelie Davidson, startled her from where she sat in the seat across from her.

She stared at Samuel's picture, her eyes glazed over. "But I can't let him go."

"You must. Your future husband deserves for you to be true to him, both in heart and in body."

Heaviness pulled her eyelids down. Tears threatened to fall, and she did not want Amelie to witness her grief. Her friend was two years older than her own age of twenty-three, a friend and companion her father had sent to travel with her to California. Because she would be on the train for most of the journey, he decided she would be safe to travel without a hired guard. Her fiancé, Harvey Mason, would meet her at the train station when they reached California.

The breath stuttered in her lungs. How could she possibly marry a man she hadn't even met? How could she possibly marry when her heart still ached?

She closed the locket, though it remained nestled inside her palm.

Finally, she opened her eyes and managed a smile. A surge of gratitude filled her for her friend's calming presence. "What would I do without you, Amelie?"

"Not much, I reckon," she teased. Amelie's expression softened as she squeezed her hand. "I know this is difficult for you. Remember that I'm here for you for however long you need me. You're the best friend I've ever had. I want you to be happy. If Mr. Mason says so much as an unkind word to you, he will have me to deal with."

She smiled past her watery eyes. She had the best friend in the entire world.

"Look over there, Nathan," a man said to his son a couple of seats in front of them. He pointed out the window, and the boy jumped up eagerly and pressed his nose to the glass. "You can see Wylder from here. Isn't it beautiful?"

She craned her neck to get a better view and smiled. Yes, this part of the Wyoming Territory was beautiful. A large mountain loomed high on one side of the tracks while sprawling green fields and sagebrush stretched endlessly on the other side. In the distance, a cluster of buildings grew larger with each passing minute.

Wylder.

What would it be like to live in a small town? Being from a big city herself, she couldn't imagine what kind of life those people lived.

The locket grew warmer within her palm as she gazed out the window. What she wouldn't give for a large dose of peace and quiet, at least until her heartache settled.

If it ever did.

She knew for certain she wouldn't find a quiet life in California. Harvey was a wealthy, influential man. He often entertained guests and joined the throngs of society. How many smiles would she have to fake before they became real?

The train lurched as it slammed on the brakes, and she braced herself when she nearly tumbled out of her seat. Deafening squeals of the brakes filled her ears.

She glanced out the window to find sparks jumping up from the wheels in a shower of orange and yellow. She clutched the arms of her seat, her heart hammering in her chest.

"What's happening, Papa?" Nathan whimpered, holding tightly to his father.

"It's likely just an animal on the tracks," he reassured.

If that were the case, the train driver would blow the horn to get the animal to move on its own accord. The horn didn't blow.

"Amelie," she said in a strained voice over the still-squealing brakes, her fingers turning white from clutching the seat so hard.

People began screaming in the car ahead of them, which set off a panic in her own car. Women clutched their children tightly. Men stood to get a better view out the window.

A gentleman swore moments before a thunderous boom echoed outside. The train jerked violently, throwing her out of her seat and onto the floor. She attempted to scramble back to the seat, but the moment she found her feet again, a screech louder than anything she'd ever experienced deafened her ears. The train's rocky movements threw her down, her head hitting the corner of a seat.

Screams. Ear-splitting screams.

The train began tipping to the side. Fear burned through her veins, panic lodged in her throat as the train jerked and rumbled, and finally it crashed onto its side.

People were tossed like rag dolls as gravity pulled on them like a puppeteer's strings. Glass shattered. Metal shrieked as if a storm's claws ripped the roof right off the train.

And then the world lay still.

Silence.

Acrid smoke burned Sophia's nostrils. She coughed and then winced at the terrible pain pounding against her skull. An aching burn raced from her head, down her shoulders, to her legs. Something sticky dripped down her face. A heavy weight crushed her against shattered glass and warped metal.

"Nathan, Nathan!" someone shouted in the deafening silence.

"I'm here, Papa," Nathan mumbled.

More people began stirring and calling out to loved ones. Others remained still.

She gasped in a breath of air as the weight lifted off her, only for horror to grip her tight when she stared back at the blank eyes of a dead man. Another man, who had lifted the body, heaved it away and helped her to unsteady feet before moving on to the next victim of the crash.

Dizziness clung tight to her skull like a stubborn grease stain. She squeezed her eyes shut, only for them to snap open again as she scanned the train car for a glimpse of red hair. Her shoes crunched against broken glass. Several unmoving bodies lay on the floor, which used to be the side of the train, now unrecognizable. Howls of pain and the cries of fearful children filled the warped space.

The burning scent of overworked brakes became stronger like a cloud of thick fog.

She took another unsteady step and paused when she caught sight of a head of red hair coated in blood.

"No." She gasped, stumbling through shards of

glass to reach her friend. "No!"

Amelie lay still as she turned her over. Green eyes stared vacantly at the ceiling, her body limp and her chest unmoving. Blood stained her hair, her clothes, and it coated the fabric of the seat nearest her.

"No!" She shook her friend's shoulders but received no response. "Amelie!" Tears escaped her eyes as she held Amelie in her arms and rocked back and forth. "Please, no. I beg you."

Still no response. Amelie remained unmoving and limp. No breath. No pulse.

She was dead.

"The train ran into a fallen tree across the tracks!" a man shouted. "Don't panic. We'll get everyone out."

With the help of several other men, he managed to pry open the door, which now lay on the top of the car. It squealed open, protesting and groaning against the rough handling. One by one, they pulled women and children out of the wreckage, and when someone reached for her, she shook her head and clung tighter to Amelie.

"We'll get her out," he said in a sympathetic tone. "I promise."

She nodded numbly and allowed him to pull her to her feet. As if she weighed nothing, he lifted her through the hole above and into another man's waiting arms. From there, he lowered her to another, who set her down on dry ground.

Dirt. Sagebrush. Broken glass. Mangled metal.

Death.

Another round of screams echoed in the afternoon sky as four men thundered by on horseback, revolvers held in the air while they shot several rounds heavenward. She flinched away from them.

But the men didn't shoot anyone. Rather, they rounded everyone up, guns pointed menacingly in their direction.

"Listen up!" One of the highwaymen pointed his revolver at each man. A bandana covered his mouth, and his hat shadowed the remainder of his face. "Hand over your valuables. Money. Jewelry. Pocket watches. Silver. Weapons. If you don't comply, you will forfeit your life."

Fear, dread, and anxiety catapulted through her as people began to comply. Panic broke through the numbness in her heart as she grabbed her locket and tucked it into her bodice to hide it. Unfortunately, the bandit leader noticed.

"You." He loosely pointed his revolver in her direction. People stepped away, giving her a wide berth to face the demon alone. "Hand it over."

Her chin trembled as she stared him in the eye. "No."

He hopped from his horse, landing with a thud in a mound of dirt. He stopped only feet away, his cold eyes tearing through her. "I said hand it over. Otherwise, I'll come and take it."

Not fear, but anger boiled up inside her. He was responsible for Amelie's death. She'd left this life far too soon over the greed of a few highwaymen.

The man growled, grabbed her wrist, and then reached for the locket.

"You will have to pry it from my cold, dead fingers!" An animal-like, guttural screech escaped her mouth as she threw herself at him, knocking him off balance until they both landed on the ground. She punched, clawed, scratched, and bit the man who had taken Amelie from her.

But all too soon, he grabbed her by the hair. Pain ripped through her scalp as he pulled her off him and smashed the butt of his gun against her temple.

The world spun as she collapsed to the ground, her limbs too weak to fight back when he grabbed her locket and snapped the chain right off her neck. She made a pathetic attempt to snatch it back but earned herself a sharp kick to the ribs as if she were a mongrel begging for a scrap of food. Pain burst through her side and transitioned to a pounding in her skull. Everything ached.

Even worse, her heart crumbled into dust until nothing remained.

Amelie—gone.

Samuel—gone.

The highwaymen finished their thieving, and Sophia watched with a heavy heart as they rode off, a cloud of dust kicking up in their wake.

"Are you all right?" someone asked as he inspected her head. Nathan's father.

Not able to find her voice, she nodded, the gesture a betrayal of what really lay within her heart.

Small specks rushed toward them from the direction of the town. People, she realized. They were coming to help.

Her feet stumbled forward, cold numbness and desperation guiding her actions despite the agony rippling through her head and ribs. Sagebrush snagged her skirts as she walked as fast as her weary feet would allow, her focus on the people growing larger with each passing second. A brisk wind urged her faster, but the quicker she walked, the more she stumbled.

She squeezed her eyes shut for a moment to try to push away the dizziness clutching her head. Her temple throbbed. Her ribs ached. Her shoulder stung.

The hoard of people from Wylder gathered around her while several continued past toward the train. Each one of them shouted over the other to be heard, and judging from their panicked looks, they'd either seen or heard the crash from the town.

"Let her breathe," someone ordered, and thankfully, everyone stepped back to give her a little more space.

"Highwaymen," she murmured.

Another round of deafening voices cascaded into her, while several more people broke away from the group toward the train.

"Wagons. We need wagons." Hopefully, someone heard her voice in the throng of shouting chaos. "People are dead." But when she spotted a horse-drawn wagon flying past, she relaxed slightly. Or was she tipping?

Her feet managed to catch her swaying body.

"Jason!" someone shouted in the fray. "Did you get a good look at them?"

Jason? I know a Jason.

From two years ago. But it couldn't possibly be the same person.

Her heart gave a start when, indeed, the same man who'd delivered such awful news a couple of years ago walked briskly to join another man. They spoke in low tones, expressions serious.

Wait a moment. The second man looked familiar. Messy brown hair. Freckles. Tall.

And then he glanced up as if he felt her gaze on

him.

Her entire world ground to a halt. Blood hardened into ice in her veins. The noise and chaos around her disappeared as she found herself gazing back into the bluest of eyes, which widened in recognition.

Her heart seemed to stop beating. Her lungs tightened and refused to draw breath. Black seeped into the corners of her vision. Dizziness tipped her one way and then the other as she swayed on unsteady feet. Her limbs grew heavy. And the last thing she was aware of was a pair of strong arms catching her before her world turned dark.

Chapter 3

"She's lost too much blood." A woman fussed as she rushed to Samuel's side and placed her hand against Sophia's face.

Shock coursed through him as he stared back at her. His heart beat in erratic rhythms. Heat in his blood spiked as comprehension tried to cut through his disbelief. His arms trembled as he cradled her against him. He stared wide-eyed at the blood matted in her dark-blonde hair and the tendrils of red dripping down her cheek. A purple bruise discolored her temple. Her face was deathly pale as if she stood on death's doorstep.

A voice cut through the fog of his daze, and he lifted his unfocused gaze to the older woman who spoke to him. "We need to put pressure on her head wound."

He blinked a couple of times before an ice-cold bucket of awareness dumped over his head. Sophia really was here. His Sophia. And she was injured.

Panic replaced his shock as he ripped out a handkerchief from his pocket and handed it to the woman while he carefully scooped Sophia into his arms. "Put pressure on this while I carry her," he ordered in a serious tone. His Sophia was hurt. Nothing else mattered at the moment. Nothing. "Where can we put her?"

The woman did as he asked and held the handkerchief against her head. "The doctor is seeing to the injured. But I have some nursing experience. She can stay with Ivan and me."

Jason joined his side as they made their way back to town on foot and approached a ranch with a modest home and barn. The journey was short, but it felt like years instead of minutes.

"Holy," Jason murmured after getting a better look at her. "Is that—"

"Yes."

A lump of dread formed in his throat, but when he tried to swallow, it refused to go down as he gazed down at her face, which seemed to grow paler by the minute.

Finally, they entered the house, and the woman, whose name he learned was Julia Pace, ushered them into one of three bedrooms on the main and only floor. He laid Sophia on the bed and took Mrs. Pace's place in holding the handkerchief as she fetched water and clean cloths.

Every memory, every regret tackled him as he gazed down at her unconscious face. Every laugh they'd shared. Every quip they'd traded. Every fight and every tender moment.

Home.

A single root dug fast into the ground beneath his feet. But no matter how hard he tried to sever it, the root remained strong and steady.

"What is she doing this far west?" Jason asked, snapping him out of his reverie. "Last I saw her, she was in New York."

Before he could answer, Mrs. Pace returned with a

pot of water and a couple of cloths.

"The poor dear." She clicked her tongue as she cleaned the cut. Sophia didn't stir, and for the dozenth time, he checked to make sure she breathed. In the end, he held on to her wrist for the constant reassurance of her pulse. Far too soon, the water was tinted red. "Did you two see what happened?"

"Every second of it."

The train had come unexpectedly early, and he hadn't reached it in time to catch McKinney before the accident. However, he'd had the perfect view from the town when it approached Wylder. He hadn't realized anything was wrong until the train slammed on its brakes. Then the crash. The derailment. The four familiar highwaymen had hidden the tree on the tracks well. He hadn't stayed to watch anymore because he'd needed to find Jason.

To think Sophia had been a passenger...

"Is she your sweetheart, dear?"

Jason coughed in the corner, but it sounded suspiciously like a snort of laughter.

Samuel glared before he answered. "No. Sophia is a friend."

"Hmm..."

Although he didn't like leaving Sophia's side, he obliged when Julia pushed the two of them out of the room to change Sophia's clothing, bandage her up, and check for any other injuries. Samuel paced back and forth across the front room, inspecting photographs of Mrs. Pace and her husband with someone who looked to be their only child. A woman around Sophia's age.

"I know this is horrible timing," Jason said beside the window, and only for a moment did Samuel stop pacing. "But what about McKinney? He got away because of your *attachment*."

Running a hand down his face, Samuel joined his friend at the window and stared out. A wagon rolled by, one filled with injured people. What a disaster. If they'd only caught the highwaymen by now, his childhood friend would be safe and uninjured.

"It's Sophia," he replied lamely. Of course, if he hadn't slipped up and called Jason by his real name, he wondered if he would have run into her at all. "Besides, McKinney will likely lie low for a little bit. He won't travel and risk getting caught by the authorities."

"Or by a couple of bounty hunters."

He nodded distractedly, his gaze drifting to the closed bedroom door. After what seemed like ages, the door opened, and Mrs. Pace exited with a red-tinted pot of water and a dress covered in blood. Dread pooled in his stomach at her grave expression.

"What is it?" His voice escaped as a raspy whisper.

Her mouth pressed tightly together. "Two head injuries, glass embedded in her skin, bruised ribs. I think on top of the accident, someone beat her as well. But judging by the amount of grime beneath her fingernails, she put up a good fight."

His hands balled into fists, anger growing hot in his bloodstream. He clenched his teeth, his entire body wanting to jump into action. He'd never wanted to kill a man more in his life than he wanted to kill McKinney.

"Is she decent? Can I see her?" Before she answered, he crossed the room in large, purposeful strides. "You know what? I don't even care. I need to see her."

He slipped inside the room and closed the door

behind him. To hell with propriety. For two children who had grown up together on the same property, despite being on different ends of wealth, they had seen each other indecent before. Such as playing in the stream together and getting drenched. Visiting one when the other was sick and stuck in bed. Sneaking into the kitchen for food in the middle of the night in night clothes.

Warmth burned in his chest at the memories of their childhood. But the heat quickly turned into ice when he laid eyes on Sophia's pale face. A white bandage wrapped around her forehead, and another poked out from the shoulder of her nightdress.

He pulled up a chair and took her hand. Far too cold for comfort. "Sophia," he murmured. "I've missed you."

No answer. Only the sound of her shallow breathing filled the small room. But with broken ribs like he assumed them to be, breathing would be a difficult endeavor.

With gentle fingers, he touched the soft, silky strands of her dark-blonde hair. He traced the curve of her jaw. If she opened her eyes, he knew he would find light-brown eyes full of life, laughter, and kindness.

A surprising skip of admiration passed over him as he took in her heart-shaped face, her smooth cheeks, her pink lips. He didn't remember her being so beautiful two years ago.

Uncomfortable with the sudden turn of thoughts, he squeezed her hand and stood. "Get better, Sophia. When you wake up, I'll make sure to bring some of those lemon drops you love so much."

Surely, the mercantile in Wylder sold lemon drops.

Giving her hand an impulsive kiss, he left the room and ignored the others' curious, watchful stares. "Thank you, Mrs. Pace, for housing her here. I'm staying at the Wylder Hotel. When she wakes—"

"I'll send for you. But I have a feeling you'll be back long before then." The older woman's eyes sparkled as if she knew something he didn't. He shrugged it off.

He placed his hat back on his head, tipped it, and he and Jason left the house. Heavy guilt settled on his shoulders, growing more burdensome with each step he took back toward town. Not until they passed the third house did he speak.

"This is my fault."

Jason shook his head. "It's not."

"If we'd caught McKinney by now, this would never have happened." He clenched his fists and didn't even attempt a wave when they passed a man riding by on his horse. "I want to kill him for this."

"I'll be your second," Jason joked, but the amusement didn't reach his eyes. They couldn't kill him if they wanted the bounty. But after the train accident, he wouldn't doubt the man would be wanted dead or alive. He hoped he wouldn't have to pull the trigger, but to protect Sophia, he would do whatever it took.

They walked down Old Cheyenne Road, which bustled with people from town and those who had been in the accident. Many people sat on the stairs of the post office as if waiting to send telegrams, some wearing slings, others with red-rimmed eyes. An inconsolable child clung to her mother and sobbed into her shoulder. They had nowhere to go. At least not until the coach arrived or until the train debris was cleared and the railroad repaired.

His horse snorted as he approached, still tied to the hitching post in front of the Five Star Saloon. He stamped his hoof impatiently, like his owner, never satisfied to stay in one place for long.

He mounted the loyal creature, turned him around, and rode in the direction of the tracks. When they neared the train, he swallowed a knot in his throat at the scene before him. The doctor ran himself ragged as he tended to the injured. Others dug through the debris of the derailed train to find the dead and lined them up several yards away.

Red hair flashed in the corner of his vision. Dread sank to the heels of his boots.

"Amelie."

She lay unmoving with the other twenty-three bodies. The young woman was his and Sophia's childhood friend, though she had been closer to Sophia. Samuel had often teased that he would marry her just to make Sophia angry, but there had never been anything between them. And to see her like this…

Swallowing another lump, he took his hat off his head and held it to his chest.

Did Sophia know?

"Ellis," Jason called, using his alias, gesturing with his head to follow him a little ways down the railroad. "Look."

A trail of hoofprints in the dirt began near the train and headed east. They followed, Jason's gaze glued to the hoofprints while Samuel watched for potential threats. They wound around a cluster of boulders, maneuvered the horses over a patch of trampled sagebrush, and entered a copse of trees.

No sign of the highwaymen anywhere.

All too suddenly, the hoofprints veered back around, leading them west once more before joining with the road and becoming unidentifiable amongst the dozens of other hoofprints and wheel tracks.

"Samuel," Jason murmured, slipping up and using his real name, his eyes wide.

"I see it."

The tracks led straight into town. Wherever McKinney and his men were lying low, it was in the one place the highwaymen likely didn't expect to be found.

Wylder.

Chapter 4

Sophia woke on and off in a daze with a raging headache, and each time, a woman named Julia tended to her until keeping her head up and her eyelids open proved to be too much. The world shifted and swirled. Eventually, keeping her eyes closed was a mercy to keep her surroundings from spinning.

When she woke again, her head still pounded, but the room no longer spun.

Julia gently pulled at the wrapping around her head. Her wrinkles deepened as she smiled. "Good. Your wound has stopped bleeding. A nasty cut on your head and an even nastier bruise on your temple. Do you remember what happened?"

Her clammy hands touched the edge of the bandage wrapped around her forehead and then moved to clasp her locket.

Except…the locket no longer hung from her neck.

A heavy weight settled on her chest as she gazed out the window. The small boy from the train, Nathan, chased a dog around the yard, laughing without a care in the world. In another life, she might have smiled. Her heart couldn't find the will.

"I remember everything."

Too much. She wished she could forget.

"You will need to pick up your trunks in town. I'm not certain if everything is still in there." Taking a deep breath, she continued. "There is also the matter of the young man who keeps asking after your health. He wishes to see you."

Panic rose to her throat, unwelcome and suffocating. "Do not let him in!"

"But Ellis has been worried sick."

"Ellis?" She grunted with the effort of pushing herself into a sitting position. "No, his name is Samuel."

The older woman shrugged. "He said it was Ellis."

Shaking her head, she thought back to when she'd made eye contact with him. Those blue eyes were unmistakable. "I know what I saw. His name is Samuel. And he's a dirty, rotten, lying, deceiving snake of a bastard!" She fell back into the pillows when her head throbbed too much to hold it up. A sudden ache welled within her. "What happened to the train's passengers?"

The woman, sweet thing she was, exchanged the used wrappings for a fresh bandage, one free of dried, crusted blood. "Most people are either staying at the hotel or Culpepper's Boarding House until the mess is cleaned up. The injured are either crowded in with the doctor or staying with others in town. Like you, dear. And little Nathan and his father, Steven. They're staying in the barn."

"And...and the dead?" she whispered.

Julia gave her hand a sympathetic pat. "There was nothing to do but bury them in the Bone Orchard Cemetery and send word to their loved ones."

Bone Orchard Cemetery.

"Your gentleman was able to identify your friend and sent a letter to her folks. I'm sorry for your loss."

"He is not my gentleman."

Gentleman was the last word she'd use to describe Samuel, especially after how he'd treated her.

With one last pat to her hand, Julia left the room, leaving Sophia to stare blankly at the wall in front of her. The room lay bare save for a single picture frame with an image on a poorly painted canvas, as if a child was the artist. A beaming sun shone over a field of grass. Flowers popped up from the base of a tall tree. A brown horse with an overly long neck reached for an apple.

Carefree. Bright. And full of hope.

But the world wasn't bright. It was dark. And all it did was take and lie and destroy.

A deep melancholy filled the room over the next several days of her recovery. She'd turned down Samuel's request to see her. *Six times*. While his face used to be the only one she ever wanted to see, she now found it to be quite the opposite.

What was going on in her fiancé's mind right now? Had Harvey heard about the accident? When she hadn't shown up at the train station, had he worried about her?

Out of all the misery surrounding the accident, she found one silver lining—a delayed marriage.

Bandages no longer wrapped around her head, she pulled a shawl around her shoulders to face the crisp, chilly morning. Clucking hens greeted her as she stepped outside and closed the door behind her. Several brown chickens pecked at pebbles on the ground while another ran across her path.

Julia exited the chicken coop with an apron full of eggs. "Where are you off to, child?"

A chill entered her bones, and she pulled her shawl tighter. "The cemetery."

"I don't think you should go alone. If you wait a few minutes, I can—"

"I would like to go by myself."

The woman paused, looking her over with a careful eye. "If you are sure."

"I am."

With the bare bones of the directions to the cemetery, she followed the dirt path leading farther outside the town to the south. Buildings became sparser, and the land transitioned from green fields to rocks and dirt and sagebrush. Tombstones and wooden crosses stuck out of the ground, marking each grave.

On the southernmost end of the graveyard lay twenty-four graves, all recently upturned with a cross marking each name. This early in the morning, she was the only person at the cemetery, for which she was grateful. She didn't want anyone to witness her grief.

Dry, yellow grass crunched beneath her feet as she walked slowly between each row of graves. She stopped short in front of a cross with a familiar name carved into the wood with familiar careful handiwork. Samuel had carved this. Had he also dug the grave?

Amelie Davidson—beloved friend and daughter

The air rushed out of her lungs. Her head spun. Her heart slowed into a dull, pained throb. The strength in her legs gave out, and she collapsed onto her knees. She dug her fingers into the freshly turned earth. Emotions within her screamed and pounded on the walls of her heart. Dirt crowded beneath her fingernails. An ache settled in her chest as if a pile of bricks lay on top of her.

Tears cascaded from her eyes, spilling down her cheeks and plopping onto the dark earth. If only Amelie had stayed in New York rather than accompanied her on the train. If only they had exchanged seats before the crash, then Sophia would be dead and her friend still alive.

She hugged herself tightly around the torso while her tears fell freely, without end. How much grief could one person handle in two years? It was too much. She couldn't do this. Not again.

Her heart grew numb, as cold as the earth beneath her fingers.

The crunch of rocks beneath a pair of shoes alerted her to someone's presence. They stopped only feet away, but she refused to lift her head.

"Sophia," Samuel's deep voice murmured.

The numbness crawled deeper within her soul. She had loved Samuel so fiercely. The way he felt about her, casting her aside without a second thought, was as plain as day. She meant nothing to him. Never had.

"I'm sorry, Sophia."

Burning embers scalded the cool numbness, fanning the flame of anger within her. Hotter. Hotter. Hotter.

"Sorry?" she shrieked, climbing to her feet only to stare back at eyes so blue. The breath got knocked out of her lungs so quickly that she took a moment to steady herself. Those eyes. She had yearned to see them again for years. She had fallen in love with them and the man they belonged to. The rich color had visited her dreams so often. "What are you sorry for, Samuel? That you left? That you made me believe you were dead?" He winced, but she wasn't finished yet. "That you are only apologizing because you got caught in your lies? I mourned you. I…I…" She swiped furious tears from her cheeks with her palm. "I don't care why you are in Wylder. Our friendship is over."

He reached out for her. "No, I don't want—"

"Don't..." She jerked away and clutched her hands to her bleeding heart, unable to finish the sentence out loud. *Don't hurt me anymore.*

"Soph, we need to talk. We need to discuss—"

"There is nothing I want to discuss with you. Ever."

Silence echoed in the space between them, heavy and filled with grief. So many unanswered questions hung in the air, answers she wasn't ready to face. If he admitted out loud to how little he cared for her, her heart could not bear such a large crack. It would crumble into small, irreparable pieces.

His expression softened, an all too familiar look that had always sent flutters through her chest. Today, her heart remained unaffected. "How are you? I was so worried you would die when I carried you to the Paces' home. I was so afraid to lose you."

"You already have," she whispered, and his expression appeared stricken with grief for a moment before it transitioned into something hard and unreadable.

Little Nathan appeared around the bend, his small feet carrying him quickly across the graveyard, his smile wide. She had never been more grateful for the boy's presence.

He ran into her arms and held on tight before he tugged on her skirt. She dipped lower and couldn't help her tearful smile as he placed a kiss on her cheek. "Papa said you needed a hug. He was right!"

Nathan laughed and ran off, completely oblivious

to the graves around him.

Samuel's expression hardened further, his arms crossed as he watched Nathan weave around graves as if he played a game. "Is he your son?"

"Yes." A sly, revengeful grin pulled up on her lips. "I'm married. He's mine."

But then his eyebrows drew together as he looked from her to the boy and back to her. "Nice try, Sophia. You weren't married two years ago when I last saw you. He has to be about three."

"He's my stepson."

"Where's your husband?"

"Umm… Right over there." Steven approached the graveyard, much slower than his son. One arm held his hat, and the other lay in a sling. She waved to the boy's father. He waved back.

"Papa!" Nathan cried and rushed into his uninjured arm. "I gave her a hug, just like you said."

"Well done." He roughed up his son's hair and lifted his head to offer her a sympathetic smile. She knew very little about him other than what Julia had mentioned. He was a widower and a schoolteacher headed west for a new job. The man was slender with a brown mustache covering his top lip, dark-brown eyes gazing at her inquisitively.

Without offering Samuel a goodbye like he had done two years prior, she approached Steven with guilt written on her face. "Forgive me," she said quietly. "I said you were my husband."

He glanced over her shoulder, a look of concern in his eyes. "Are you in trouble? Is that man bothering you?"

Despite her resolve, tears pricked her eyes. "Not in

the way you think."

"Oh," he murmured. "Oh, I see." Then louder, he said, "Come along, dear. You need to get some rest." He placed a hand on the small of her back and led her away. She glanced over her shoulder to find Samuel staring after them, his jaw clenching, unclenching, and clenching again. He didn't follow.

After a minute of silence, instead of asking about Samuel, Steven said, "Julia told me you were headed to the cemetery. I didn't want you to be alone. I've been there before when Louise died. It was a hard thing to face alone and with a newborn to care for while I was forced to grieve."

"I'm sorry about your wife. She must have been wonderful."

"She was." His expression became somber, his eyes far away. "It was a short marriage, but I had never been happier."

Nathan ran ahead when they reached the ranch, and the dog quickly joined him. After the walk to and from the cemetery, her head began spinning again. She sank onto a porch step and rested her pounding head against the railing. Steven joined her, several feet between them.

The sun just barely made its entrance, beams of light bringing a new day to Wylder when he spoke. "May I ask about the cemetery?"

He certainly wasn't talking about Amelie.

Usually, she would have confided in Samuel or Amelie, but each was infinitely out of reach. She shrugged, facing away from him. "My life is a mess. I'm fake married to you. I'm engaged to a man I've never met. And I'm in love with a man who lied to me

41

and shattered my heart. Tell me what to do, Steven. Please."

He chuckled. "Well, I'm not sure I'll ever be ready to remarry, so you can take me off your list. I mean no offense." When she turned to face him, she mimicked his smile, her spirits buoyed with amusement. "Which leaves your betrothed and the man you love. Are you going to choose?"

"There is nothing to choose. I'm engaged. Samuel cares nothing for me."

"Nothing?" He lifted an eyebrow high before busying himself by adjusting his sling. "Tell me, Miss Meadows. Does someone who doesn't care visit twice a day to check on your welfare? Or spend hours digging the hole for your friend and carving her grave marking? Someone who doesn't care wouldn't be jealous over you finding a *husband*."

Jealous? No.

"The bastard faked his own death and let me believe it for two years. Forgive my language."

Surprise flashed across his eyes. He stroked his mustache as if deep in thought, his eyebrows furrowed. "Do you know why he did it?"

"No. And I don't think I can face the answer."

Thankfully, he changed the subject. "Have you sent word to your family? Your fiancé? A telegram would reach them the quickest."

"All my money was stolen from my luggage. I've been holding on to the hope that Harvey will inquire into why I haven't arrived yet."

"I have some I can lend you."

"No, no. Julia sent a couple of letters for me. It will be slower, but it will get there. You are too kind, Mr.

Bailey."

"Anything to help." He pulled himself to his feet with one hand, wincing as if the strain pulled on his broken arm. Before returning to the barn, he smiled. "Life flashes by faster than you know it. People come and go from your life in the blink of an eye. I've learned not to waste time on tears and rather do something with myself, with my life. It's fine to grieve. But don't let the grief take over your life. I hope you find happiness, Miss Meadows."

She watched him leave, her heart lighter than minutes before. The last two years had been filled with death and mourning and misery. She wanted to be happy again. For herself. For Amelie. For her future. Although she wasn't quite sure how to achieve it, she wanted to start now. One small step at a time.

Picking herself up off the step and ignoring the ache in her head, she went to find Julia.

Chapter 5

"Will you stop glowering?" Jason kicked Samuel's foot beneath the table. "You're going to scare away potential wives, and you're making *me* unapproachable."

Samuel rolled his eyes and shifted his attention from the patrons at the Five Star Saloon to stare at his friend. The man's hair looked neater today, his clothes clean and tidy. "You're looking for a wife? Here? Why would you want to settle in Wylder?"

"Why not? It's as good a place as any. Cozy in a small town kind of way. The people are nice. Most of them, at least. It's a perfect opportunity to make something of myself. A change of occupation."

His mouth quirked to the side as he pondered Jason's words. Over the last two years, they'd traveled from town to town, never settling or laying down roots. For the first time, Samuel had found a place that had begun to feel like home, likely because of Sophia's presence.

Jason snapped his fingers in his face, forcing his attention away from the chip in the wooden table. "You're doing it again. Why are you glowering so much?"

"I'm not."

However, his friend raised a disbelieving eyebrow.

His gaze roamed over the saloon again, taking in

the talking and laughing patrons enjoying their dinner. A few people looked familiar from when he'd seen them around town, but none were the faces he wanted to see, the men he wanted to beat senseless.

Several delicious smells wafted in the air, from salted pork to venison stew, mingling with the loud hum of conversation. He watched the patrons at the bar for a moment before his gaze slid over the piano tucked in the corner. Since his arrival, he hadn't heard anyone playing it. Sophia would love it. She could do wonders with a few keystrokes.

His frown made a reappearance. "Sophia is married. I'm not sure why it bothers me so much. Of course, I expected her to move on with her life and me with mine, but… I just wasn't prepared for it."

"Same thing happened to me, but it was my sister. She got married when I was off on a job, and suddenly my relationship with her was different. We rarely write to each other anymore now that she has her own family to worry about. The shock will wear off, and you'll find a way to adjust."

"I'm not sure I will," he murmured as he turned his glass of water between his palms.

The familiar ache associated with Sophia settled in his chest. A strange man had ripped his sense of home right from beneath him like a slippery rug tossing him onto his back. Someone else had stolen his home. Now he had nothing.

Restlessness settled in his legs, itching for him to move, the only buffer to keep him from dwelling on the ache for long. He stood and exited the establishment, Jason at his heels.

The sunset broke over Wylder in a gorgeous array

of orange, pink, and yellow, bathing the town in a beautiful golden pool of color. He exhaled a breath of awe and, for the first time, found something worth pursuing in Wylder. For a brief flicker of a moment, he wanted to settle down with a family of his own. But then his restless legs urged him forward once more, needing something to do, desperately wanting something to do.

A man swore under his breath, and Samuel's attention snapped in the direction of the alley behind the Longhorn Saloon across the street. A man with chin-length black hair, long pink scratch marks across his face, and sideburns stared back at him with wide eyes before bolting in the other direction.

"Cade McKinney," he growled before giving chase.

Dust kicked up behind him in his pursuit. He pumped his legs harder, faster, as he dodged carts and wagons. A few wandering chickens squawked and scattered as he ran past. His gaze remained glued to the black coat flying behind his bounty. Though he itched to draw his gun, he kept his fingers from reaching for the weapon.

McKinney took a sharp left turn down Buckboard Alley, and when Samuel made the same turn, he slowed in confusion when the fleeing man in black disappeared into the crowd as if vanishing into thin air.

A pile of black cloth caught his attention on the side of the road. He approached cautiously and toed the fabric with his boot.

McKinney's coat.

His gaze darted back and forth across the street with no results. The man was gone.

"You find him?" Jason asked a few moments later, out of breath.

"No, but I found this."

He bent to pick up the discarded coat. Seconds! He'd missed the man by seconds. If he'd focused on something other than his coat, he might have caught the elusive highwayman.

Jason took the coat from him and inspected it, turning out each pocket. Two pockets contained receipts from the mercantile. Another pocket held a pocket watch. And the last item…

His throat constricted when Jason held up his palm, a silver locket lying across his fingers. He recognized it immediately as the piece of jewelry he'd carried around for an entire year before faking his death.

"Sophia kept it all this time?" The warm metal greeted him as he picked up the chain and dangled the locket in front of his face. "I'm not sure what to think," he admitted. "Is she mad at me or not?"

"A question best saved for another day." Jason clapped him on the shoulder. "You were right. McKinney is still in Wylder. What are we gonna do?"

A squeak of wagon wheels passed by them, slow and unhurried as if the driver was completely oblivious to the danger threatening the town.

"The only thing we can do—involve the sheriff. As much as I don't want to share the bounty, I don't want anyone else to die if we can prevent it. Enough people have lost their lives as it is." His thoughts turned to Amelie. A funeral for those killed in the train wreck was to be held tomorrow in the late afternoon. He would be there. No matter what.

He remained on the lookout for McKinney and his

gang on their way to the sheriff's office. When they arrived, the front door lay open as if in invitation to enter. A man sat at a desk, his expression haggard and his lips pressed tight together. He glanced up from the papers scattered about his desk and eyed them with careful scrutiny.

"I've seen the two of you around town," he said. "You arrived only a day before the train accident."

Samuel grimaced as he held out his hand to shake his. The man grasped it with a strong grip. "Samuel Woods."

"What—" Jason started to protest, but he cut across him.

"There's no point in using my alias anymore. Sophia already knows."

The sheriff stood, his expression serious as he looked from their faces to the guns sitting on their hips and toward the door as if sizing up the situation. But still, he replied, "Sheriff Branch Wylder. What's going on?"

He swallowed and glanced toward the door. Anyone could pass by and overhear them, so he closed the door, only to be met by an even more serious, more threatening face from the sheriff than before.

"Sheriff," he began, moving to the window to glance outside. Still no sign of McKinney. Obviously, he would make a point to avoid the sheriff in town. "We are bounty hunters. We've been chasing a man and his gang, highwaymen, for months. We heard they were headed to Wylder. Something about a train. We didn't realize…" He ran a hand down his face as he crossed the room and gazed at the wanted posters pinned to the wall. He recognized a rudimentary drawing of

McKinney, ripped it off the wall, and handed it to the sheriff. "We didn't catch them in time. But we just ran into their leader five minutes ago."

Branch's entire body stiffened with alertness as he placed his hand on the gun in his holster. "They're here? In town? I thought they would have moved on already."

Jason shook his head, his arms folded over his chest. "Sometimes, the best place to hide is in plain sight."

The sheriff ran a hand over his mustache. "You're sure you saw him?"

Samuel answered. "Positive. Gave him a good chase around town too."

Nodding, Branch paced the small space behind his desk. "We'll catch these bastards, but I don't want to cause a panic. We'll do it quietly. Where did you last see McKinney?"

"Buckboard Alley." Jason placed the black coat on the desk. "He left behind his coat, a couple of receipts, and two stolen items."

"Let's see them."

Handing over the locket created an anxious strain in his shoulders. He needed it. He wasn't ready to give it up. Not even to Sophia. Eventually, he knew he needed to return the piece of jewelry, but right now, he wanted it near him.

Sheriff Wylder took a moment to look over the receipts. "I'll inquire discreetly at the mercantile, find out if Finn remembers anything. He has to be staying somewhere. I'll ask a few trusted friends to keep a lookout as well. See if you two can find anything around Culpepper's or the hotel."

49

"He was hanging around the Longhorn Saloon," Jason added.

Again, the sheriff nodded with a serious look. "If he was with the ladies, they don't give away client information. I'll let you inquire at the bar, Mr...."

"Smith. Jason Smith."

"We need to catch these men and put them where they belong before they leave town." The sheriff inspected the pocket watch before he took the locket and opened it. He stilled as his gaze slowly lifted to look Samuel over.

"Where did you say you got this locket?"

"It belonged to my friend." Samuel shifted uncomfortably from one foot to the other under his scrutiny. "She was on the train during the accident. We found it in the coat."

The man looked him up and down again. "She was going to meet you?"

"No. I'm not sure where she was headed. We haven't seen each other in a couple of years."

"Hmm… Well, if she survived the accident, I think you have a serious problem on your hands."

He handed the open locket to him, and the moment he glanced at it, his heart stilled. An icy chill traveled up his veins when he found not only Sophia's familiar picture inside the locket but his own next to it.

No, no, no.

He ran his hands through his hair. If McKinney had this locket, and if he'd looked inside, he would connect the two of them. Sophia was in danger just by association with him.

"I need to find Sophia." He gasped before he shouldered his way out the door.

Saddling his horse where he'd left it at the livery would take too long, so he made his way across town on foot. When he arrived at the Paces' home, he pounded on the door. No answer.

He rounded the house and checked in the barn. A cow lowed at him, but he otherwise found nothing but a stack of hay, luggage, and a blanket spread over a pile of straw.

His heart raced faster and faster after each place he searched for her—the cemetery, the fields, the mercantile, and the saloon. When he found himself standing outside of Jake's Place, he shoved several breaths in and out of his lungs and attempted to keep his panic at bay. Wylder might not be a big city, but it was large enough to make finding someone difficult.

He took a deep breath to steady his pulse before he entered the establishment. A low hum from diners lifted into the air, quieter than the ruckus at the Five Star Saloon. Patrons sat at tables, enjoying their dinner. And at one of the tables…

At the sight of Steven Bailey sitting by his lonesome near the corner of the room, heat spiked in his blood. Anger crawled down his arms and into his fists. The collar at his neck suddenly became suffocatingly hot.

Not bothering to stuff down his anger, he stalked toward the man and slapped his hands down on the table. "Where's your wife?" he growled.

Several patrons glanced their way as if bracing for a fight. By the way his blood heated, he was bracing himself as well. For what reason? He wasn't sure. He only knew he was angry.

Steven paused for a moment in an infuriatingly

calm manner before he resumed stirring a sugar cube into his tea. He took a long sip and finally lifted his gaze. "You care for Sophia."

"Of course I do. We grew up together. She's my friend."

"Only a friend?"

"What else would she be?"

A flicker of a smile appeared, then disappeared just as quickly. "Well, it seems she has no interest in your friendship. What else do you have to offer?"

"What else?" He wanted to bash the man's face in for no real good reason. What was wrong with him? He flexed his fingers to coax the violent thoughts away. "She won't let me get a word in when I try to talk to her. I have nothing more to offer than an apology."

Mr. Bailey absently stirred his tea, took a sip, and set it back down on a place mat embroidered with cows. An empty plate sat at the corner of the place mat, next to perfectly lined utensils. "You hurt her deeply. Perhaps you might try to earn back her trust."

"But how?" He shook his head, wondering how the conversation had transitioned from him desperately trying to locate Sophia to him trying to earn back her favor.

"That's not something I can tell you, but rather you need to figure it out for yourself."

The other man finished his tea, left a tip on the table, and Samuel followed him to the door. Before he exited Maggie's, he turned back with a glint in his eye. "My beloved wife died in childbirth; bless her beautiful soul. Miss Meadows is not my wife. But I don't care to see her so distraught."

"Not your wife?" He blinked several times as he

processed the new information. Sophia lied to him? Why? "She's not married, then?"

"No."

A burst of relief washed through him. The place he called home was still intact, but only barely. If he didn't find a way to repair his friendship with Sophia, it would disintegrate into dust and scatter with the wind.

He welcomed the second root to shoot out from his feet and latch tightly to the earth. He needed the connection to tether him to Sophia, craved it, even.

"As for her whereabouts…" A bell tinkled overhead as Mr. Bailey opened the door. "Mr. and Mrs. Pace took her and my little Nathan to the Medicine Bow River. They should be back by now. It was good to officially meet you, Mr. Woods."

A grimace crinkled the corners of his eyes as he took the man's offered hand and shook it. "Likewise. I apologize for…" He scratched his head and glanced back to the table someone began clearing.

"Think nothing of it. I hope to see you around again before I leave Wylder."

The man left, and Samuel wandered out of the café, distracted by his thoughts. Sophia would be safe with the Paces. Until the funeral tomorrow, he needed to be vigilant. They would catch McKinney and his gang, as they had nowhere to go without being seen first. And he preferred they finish the job sooner than later.

It was time to meet up with the sheriff to find out what he learned from Finn at the mercantile.

Chapter 6

Not again.

Sophia reached for her locket but lowered her hand when she realized once more it no longer hung from her neck. She listened to the funeral proceedings with half an ear, finding it difficult for her heart to keep up with her mind.

A small bouquet of wildflowers rested in her hand as she gazed out over the rows of graves. Twenty-four new graves.

The minister continued speaking about the cycle of life and death in the grand scheme of life. Many townsfolk attended the funeral, along with most of the people involved in the train crash. Mr. Bailey and Nathan stood supportively on one side of her and the Paces on the other. She refused to meet Samuel's gaze despite his efforts to catch her eye.

One by one, the minister called out each name of the deceased, and when he said, "Miss Amelie Davidson," the pain in her heart threatened to squeeze the life from her.

She placed her bouquet of flowers at the base of the wooden cross, took a step back, and stared blankly at what remained of her dear friend. Her chin trembled, followed by the blur of gathering tears.

Her pulse jumped in surprise when someone threaded their fingers through hers and gave her hand a comforting squeeze. She swiped at the moisture in her eyes, only to gaze back at a sea of empathetic blue. Although Samuel spoke no words, his sorrowful expression mimicked hers. Amelie had been his friend as well. He needed comfort just as much as she did.

All feelings of resentment placed aside, she returned the squeeze to his hand, and together they stood in front of Amelie's grave in silence. Mr. Bailey's words echoed in her mind. *"It's fine to grieve. But don't let the grief take over your life."*

She'd succumbed to grief once, and she refused to do it a second time. But to find happiness again? It seemed so far out of reach.

Tears blurred her vision once more. Samuel released her hand, and for a moment, she felt cold and empty before his arm wrapped around her shoulders and pulled her close. A comforting warmth enveloped her as she allowed the embrace. Despite the resentment, despite the anger, his presence warmed her, healed her, provided her strength.

A familiar flicker of love lit within her heart.

She might have willed it away if she'd had enough strength, but instead, she found herself melting into him, desperate for his consoling touch.

Relief flooded through her as she turned into his side and breathed in the familiar scent of earthy forest and unbridled adventure. The trust between them lay in shards at their feet, but he was alive. She couldn't be more grateful to see him at least one last time.

Evening began to fall as everyone left the cemetery until only a few remained. Sophia reluctantly pulled away from him and followed after the Pace couple, though he quickly fell into step beside her. A hundred ideas to send him away floated through her mind, and when they reached the ranch, she turned to him…but every single idea fled.

She gazed back at him in the waning light of dusk. One single look from his beautiful blue eyes stirred old feelings. Her heart beat fast. Her stomach tied into knots. The photo in her locket didn't do him justice. He was more handsome than she remembered.

"Can I stay a little longer?" he asked after the others disappeared inside. His gaze turned to the skies. "It's a beautiful evening. Wouldn't want it to go to waste."

A refusal lay on the tip of her tongue, but when she opened her mouth, the wrong word escaped. "Yes."

She climbed a porch step and paused. More than likely, she could still take it back. But then she climbed another and then another before she settled on the porch swing. He lowered himself next to her. Too close but not close enough.

"Your husband won't mind, will he?" Samuel asked, a challenging eyebrow raised.

"What?"

"Your husband. I don't want him to get the wrong idea."

Oh, right. The lie about Mr. Bailey. If Samuel thought the widower was her husband, he must have thought it strange they hadn't talked much or comforted each other during the funeral.

With a sigh, she leaned back against the slats of wood and gazed up at the streaks of orange and pink in the skies above. Crickets chirped a soothing chorus around them. A couple of chickens sauntered across the yard, pecking at rocks in search of a bite to eat.

"Mr. Bailey is not my husband. I met him on the train."

"Why did you lie?"

The question came far too quickly as if he'd been prepared to ask it. Had he known already?

She turned her head to look more fully at him, only to be pierced by a pair of serious eyes—an expression she'd seen far too often. Anger. Defiance. Worry. And something she didn't quite recognize.

Her reply was far calmer than what she wanted to shout at him. "You have some nerve getting upset with me for lying, Sam. Have you ever mourned someone before? Truly mourned? Do you know how much it hurts?"

He glanced away, his expression guilty as he likely thought of the parents he'd lost. His mother to sickness. His father to a stagecoach accident.

Instead of answering her question, he hung his head and leaned forward to brace his elbows on his knees as they slowly rocked back and forth on the swing.

A heavy ache settled on her chest. She wasn't ready to face his reason for leaving. She couldn't bear the hurt. But when she tried to slide off the swing, Samuel spoke with a small smile on his face.

"Amelie always tattled on us as children." He chuckled.

She returned to her seat, her mouth quirking up in amusement at the fond memories. "We *did* hide from her often so we could get into mischief without getting in trouble. Remember the time with the mud pit?"

His deep laughter sent shivers of awareness up her arms. "I thought we were successful in ditching her. I can't say I loved the condescending look your father gave us when Amelie pulled him outside."

"It was a fun mud pit."

"Or the time when I dared you to ride backward in the saddle? I don't think I've ever seen your father more furious."

"To be fair, it was a stupid dare."

He playfully nudged her arm with his elbow. "You never could resist a dare."

Her mouth already hurt from smiling. The last time she had smiled this much had been a long time ago. "Oh, Amelie. Always followed the rules, but she was the kindest person I've ever known."

He nodded. "Always the first to bake sweets for someone in need."

"The first to volunteer to help an ailing mother."

"The first to organize charities." The swing's chains rattled as they continued to rock in silence, at least until he smiled again. "My family wasn't wealthy like yours or Amelie's, so I didn't get the education my mother always wanted for me. Amelie was smart and kind enough to tutor me in mathematics. She knew far more than I did despite being a year younger than me."

A year younger.

She fiddled with a ruffle on her blouse. She and Samuel were three years apart in age. Not for the first time, she wondered if the age gap was why he'd never expressed interest in her romantically.

"You often teased me about you someday marrying Amelie." She now fiddled with a seam on her skirt. "You must be upset about losing the opportunity."

His shoulders shook as he laughed, and when he turned his head to meet her gaze, heat climbed up her neck and into her hairline. Holy handsome. His smile caused her heart to tremble.

"You were fun to tease. Your reactions were—" Samuel paused as his smile turned into a playful smirk. "Over the top."

"They were not."

"Yes, they were. When I threatened to read your diary, you tackled me into the fountain. When I stole every matching pair of your stockings, you snuck into my room while I was sleeping and cut chunks of my hair off with scissors."

Laughter escaped her mouth, and she tried to muffle it with her hand. "Oh, I remember that. Your mother was livid for making you look ugly for a good couple of months. I apologized at least a dozen times."

The smile on his face remained as he shook his head in exasperation. "As much as I miss Amelie and the times the three of us shared, marrying her was never in my plans. She would have made an awful wife for me. I couldn't live under such a ruling thumb, and she would have hated my need for adventure."

Another stretch of silence fell between them. The sunset streaks in the sky transitioned into a blanket of midnight blue, with twinkling stars stretched endlessly in every direction. Crickets continued to chirp in a unified rhythm, filling the tense yet comforting quiet in the inches between her and Samuel.

"The atmosphere is beautiful out here," she murmured, keeping her gaze fixed to the sky rather than him. "You can't see as many stars in New York."

He turned to her so their knees nearly brushed. "Why were you on that train, Sophia? Just you and Amelie?"

She couldn't decide if putting another wedge between them was a good thing or bad. On the one hand, she enjoyed his company. On the other, she feared it would never last. The hurt and broken trust between them was too great.

Staring into her lap, she answered, "I am the oldest of four daughters. Someone needed to marry well. My father arranged a marriage for me to Harvey Mason, a wealthy man living in California. I was on my way to meet him. And get married."

More silence. Heavy. Deafening.

She risked a glance in his direction to find his jaw clenching and unclenching in sync with his fists.

"Congratulations," he finally said in a strained voice. "On your engagement."

An answer refused to grace her lips. She was not particularly excited herself, but to say as much would be unkind and unnecessary.

The reminder of Harvey added yet another wedge between them. Amelie had been right. She couldn't be married to one man and still wear another man around her neck. Cutting ties with Samuel would be best. No matter how much her heart ached to do it.

"You should go," she whispered.

He stood and leaned against the wooden railing, a foot on the porch step. "Can I call on you tomorrow?"

"No. Good night, Sam."

She started to open the front door but stopped when he called after her. "I'll see you at the ceilidh tomorrow night, then. Some Irish folks are holding a dance in their barn."

"I can't dance right after Amelie died. It's not right."

"She would want you to be happy. Do it for her. For our friend."

A lump formed in her throat as she paused at his invitation. She wanted to be happy again. But did she have any right? When Amelie lay six feet beneath the ground, could she dance knowing her friend would never dance again?

Something rattled behind her, and she turned to find him shaking a paper bag.

Her eyes widened.

"I hoped I wouldn't have to resort to bribery, but here we are." A mischievous smile spread across his face. "If I remember correctly, you are rather fond of lemon drops. Would this entice you to stop by for a few minutes?"

She placed her hands on her hips, a stern look on her face. "You play dirty, Samuel."

"Not as dirty as you. It's only a matter of time before the queen of dirt takes her throne."

Laughter burst from her as she took the bag from him and popped one of the yellow candies into her mouth. The sweet, acidic taste washed over her tongue and brought her back to happier days filled with warmth and sunshine. Days of sitting beneath a shady tree beside Samuel as they talked and traded sweets. Life had been so simple back then.

"Care to share?" he asked, breaking her out of her memories as he leaned against the railing and crossed his arms. He cast her a roguish grin.

His playful mood spurred her own. "You want one?" She reached into the bag and pulled out a single lemon drop. "Then I dare you to come and get it."

As if she were a child again, she teasingly placed

the candy between her teeth. When she'd done it in the past, he'd made a disgusted face and settled for another sweet, but disgust didn't flash across his face as she'd expected. Not even playful disgust. Instead, his eyes darkened, his throat bobbing up and down as he swallowed.

Her heart raced as he unfolded his arms and crossed the space between them. She backed up against the door but otherwise held her ground as she gazed into his eyes. Calloused yet gentle fingers cupped her chin and tipped her head upward, the starry night sky a backdrop to his silhouette.

Every fiber of her thrummed alive at his touch. Her heart fluttered in her ribcage. He'd never looked at her like this before. Ever.

He leaned closer, and just when she thought he might kiss the candy right from her mouth, he plucked it out with his fingers instead and popped it into his mouth with a grin.

The teasing devil.

"See you at the ceilidh." He descended the stairs with a final wave goodbye without turning around. " 'Night, Soph."

She watched him leave, her pulse pounding in her ears faster than she thought possible. Two years certainly weren't enough to put her feelings behind her. They were stronger than ever, and she wasn't sure what to do about it.

Chapter 7

"By Harry," Jason murmured. "You almost kissed her?"

Samuel nodded distractedly as he saddled his horse the next day. His fingers moved deftly, having done this hundreds of times before. He pulled the front cinch tighter the moment his horse let out a breath before he strapped the flank cinch.

He and Jason walked their horses down the livery and into the afternoon sunlight. A cool breeze whispered past, foretelling of a turn in the weather.

"I'm not sure what compelled me. She's different. I'm different. But still the same." He clenched his fist and pounded it lightly on the saddle. His horse snorted and flicked his tail at him in annoyance. "It's not like I haven't thought about kissing her before, as any adolescent boy might about any female. But this time was different." Letting out a sigh, he leaned against his horse as he stared out over the rough terrain just outside town. "Let's get moving. Those two will return any minute now."

They mounted their horses and trotted down the trail leading out of the west side of town. A large smile grew across Jason's face. "After today, only half the problem will remain."

Samuel gave his friend an affirmative nod. "There's nowhere McKinney can go without us recognizing him first."

"Unless you get distracted by a beautiful woman," Jason pointed out.

"You're one to talk. You've been looking for a wife since day one of arriving in Wylder."

"You want to marry Sophia?"

"I didn't say that. I only said I almost gave in to my desire to kiss her." He ran a hand over his face and sighed. "I'm so confused. Why now? I've known her all my life. So why now when she's out of reach?"

"Is she?"

"She's engaged."

But at least she wasn't married as he'd previously thought.

They paused their conversation for a moment as the trail became smaller. He slowed down to follow behind Jason, and sped up to ride beside him when the trail widened enough for two.

"Engagements can be broken." Jason ducked beneath the overhanging branch of a pine tree.

"I don't want to settle down. And I'm the last person she would want to settle with."

"What are you going to do? Run around and catch bandits for the rest of your life? You've never wanted a wife? Children? A home?"

Home. Sophia was his home. As soon as she married, his home would disappear forever.

He thought back to the almost kiss last night, the way she'd nearly melted his resolve with a single look. They were friends, for Pete's sake. So why couldn't he stop thinking about whether her kiss would taste like sweet flowers or lemon drops?

He needed to stop this before it had a chance to

begin. If he ruined their friendship, he feared he would lose her forever. "Like I said, I'm the last person she'd want to settle down with. We're not good for each other. She's...she's... And I'm..."

Jason raised an eyebrow so high it disappeared beneath the brim of his hat. "Can't think of anything, can you? Does she know about the reason you faked your death?"

"No. I want her to ask. Otherwise, I'm not sure how to bring it up. She hasn't asked." He snapped his fingers and grinned. "I'm not a high society, influential, wealthy man. See? I'm wrong for her."

The realization punched a hole through his gut. Again, what was wrong with him? He'd known her all his life. He'd never had any romantic feelings for her. Until recently.

But was it so wrong to want something more than friendship with his life-long friend? And so suddenly too?

Before he had a chance to ponder on the feelings stirring within his heart, he focused on the task at hand. His heart pounding against his ribcage, he veered off on one side of the road and stopped his horse behind enough foliage to hide them from view. Jason did the same on the other side of the road. His friend's horse stamped its hooves excitedly, knowing from experience what they were about to do. His own horse remained still and patient.

Only a few minutes passed before a cloud of dirt traveled in their direction. The two riders they waited for rode fast. He released a breath of relief. The tip from Finn Wylder proved correct.

He picked up the coiled rope from where it draped

over the pommel of his saddle. He held tight onto one end of the rope and positioned his arm over his head in preparation to throw the other end across the road.

"Steady now, boy," he murmured as he patted the horse's neck.

Pounding hoofbeats moved closer in tune with the furious dirt clouds.

Steady.

Steady.

Steady.

He threw the other end of the coiled rope across the dirt road to Jason, who caught it, and braced himself. Samuel's gloved hands tightened their grip on the rope. His thighs squeezed his saddle while he leaned backward with his feet securely in his stirrups.

The two men couldn't stop their horses fast enough when they noticed the rope. One tried to duck beneath it, but both smashed into it while their horses ran under. The sudden impact against the rope threw them from their mounts and onto the dirt road.

Samuel dropped his end of the rope and produced a smaller, skinnier one from his saddlebag. He hopped from his horse and rushed toward one scrambling onto his hands and knees while Jason took care of the other one. He drew his gun, pulled back the hammer, and placed the barrel against the Native American's head.

The man froze.

"Forfeit all your weapons, Machk, and come willingly. You will not like what happens if you make this harder than it needs to be."

Machk glared at him with dark-brown eyes as he pulled out a gun and two knives, tossing them to the side of the road into a pile of sagebrush. He continued to glare as Samuel tied his wrists together in front of him, then tied either end of the rope from his saddle to the rope that tied the second man, Leon Riley, to Jason's saddle.

They made quick work of the task of collecting the discarded weapons before they started back toward town at a much slower pace than before. A jolt of excitement flooded his veins. Finally, after months, they'd caught two of the men in McKinney's gang. Not only would they receive the bounty for their capture, but they might obtain information on McKinney's whereabouts.

A sudden discomfort tied his stomach into a jungle of knots. What if Sophia saw him ride through town with his bounty? If she didn't, then someone else would. Word would get back to her.

Was he ready to face her after the stream of lies he'd told her in the past?

Shaking the thought away, he glanced back to find the two disgruntled men, on foot, fighting to keep up with the horses, but they didn't try to escape. Not with Jason's gun pointed in their direction as motivation to behave.

Upon reaching the town, they received many stares as they rode past. People who'd once looked at him curiously now stared at him with caution. Several children watched in awe.

They dismounted in front of the sheriff's office and towed their captives inside. Sheriff Wylder motioned them toward the jail cells and locked both behind bars.

A weight lifted off Samuel's shoulders as they returned to the office. Only a portion of the weight he carried, but enough to give him hope. Sophia was halfway to safety. Amelie was halfway to justice.

"Leon and Mute Machk," the sheriff said, nodding his head in the direction of the jail. "That's them, all right. I don't reckon I'll get anything from Machk. But Leon might talk. I'll let you know what I learn. Come back tomorrow. I'll have your bounty money ready."

"Good luck," Samuel said, his arms crossed. "Leon is a stubborn mule. But any information you can glean will be helpful. We want McKinney behind bars just as much as you do."

"Good. I hope it won't be long now."

Jason tipped his hat. "A pleasure, Sheriff." They left and mounted their horses. "How long until McKinney finds out his men are in jail?"

Judging by the whispering townsfolk glancing in their direction, not long. "Too soon. Don't let your guard down. He'll likely try something stupid out of desperation to get out of town."

"And Sophia and the locket? Is she in danger?"

He pulled his hat lower over his forehead in an attempt to hide from curious stares. "I've been looking out for her. Nothing seems amiss, so I don't think he connects her to me. I think it's best if I keep my distance from her for now."

His friend snorted, a grin growing across his face. "Uh-huh. And does keeping your distance involve skipping out on the ceilidh?"

"Yes."

"You are an idiot. You might as well escort her to California and hand her over to her fiancé while you're at it."

He clenched his fingers tight around the reins. Finally, he recognized the feeling for what it was, for what it had been since the moment he'd laid eyes on Mr. Bailey. Jealousy. White, hot jealousy. Whoever this fiancé was, he wanted to punch the man in the throat.

Taking a deep breath, he forced his fingers to relax. "Fine. One ceilidh, and that's it."

****

Samuel glanced toward the open barn doors for the dozenth time since his arrival. Perspiration slicked his palms. His heart raced as quickly as the fiddler's bow in the corner of the barn.

He wiped his hands on his trousers when Sophia still didn't show. Why was he so nervous? He'd been around Sophia plenty of times. Wanting to kiss her had been a fluke, a direct result of a romantic atmosphere and longing for his friend after so long of being apart—which he would prove if she would only walk through those doors so he didn't have to wonder anymore.

A tin whistle joined in with the fiddle, followed by the pipes to create lively music blaring across the barn. A couple dozen dancers filled the large space as they danced a line dance in unison. Jason twirled a partner by the waist before he turned to the woman across from him and skipped forward and back. The largest grin lay plastered on the man's face as he enjoyed himself.

Just when he thought Sophia had broken their agreement as he'd originally planned to, a head of dark-blonde hair walked into the barn.

Samuel's heart flopped like a fish on land as his gaze roamed over her heart-shaped face, her slender neck, and down the ruffly light-blue dress she wore, one with a slight bustle in the back.

Heat climbed his neck as she scanned the barn, only to meet his gaze after a moment. Well, shoot. It seemed as if a dusty old candle had been lit within him, and its light only grew brighter rather than dimmed.

He snapped his eyes shut to break the spell. No, he absolutely could not be falling for his friend. It only complicated matters and confused him.

But as he approached and took her hand, his heart squeezed excitedly at the contact. He knew it was already too late to stop whatever this was. At least on his end.

Guilt formed a lump in his throat. Sophia was engaged to someone else. Could he truly live with himself for coming between her and happiness with the man? Was it wrong to try to woo someone else's future bride?

"You came." He breathed.

She smiled. It was a smile he'd seen thousands of times, but this time, it sent a shiver of excitement down his spine. "If I remember correctly, somebody bribed me with lemon drops." Her expression fell into uncertainty as she touched her skirt and swayed back and forth while watching it move around her. "I wasn't sure what to wear. My city dresses aren't very suitable for the wild west."

"You look beautiful. Perfect."

Their gazes locked, and the spell fell over him again. He fought against the new root taking place but welcomed it at the same time. If any other roots secured him to the ground, he felt certain he would never be able to break free from their deep grasp.

But did he want to?

He pulled her in the direction of the wall to avoid other people coming to join the festivities and those still dancing. His attention remained rapt on the woman who had turned his life upside down in a matter of seconds.

"So…" He nonchalantly leaned against the wall and coughed into his hand. "Your fiancé. You really haven't met him before?"

She shrugged and leaned against the wall as well. But as if thinking better of it, she pushed away, brushed her skirt off, and turned her attention to the dancers. "Perhaps once at a social function years ago. But I can't say I remember him or know who he is."

"He must be beside himself with worry over the train wreck. I'm sure you're eager to meet him." He raised an eyebrow and glanced sideways at her to gauge her reaction. No reaction. Only a blank face.

Again, she shrugged one of her slender shoulders. "As eager as one is to perform a strenuous chore."

The candle within his heart flamed brighter with hope. Hope for what? He wasn't entirely sure. "You don't want to marry him?"

Anxiety passed across her face, and she reached for her neck as if to touch a necklace but then lowered her hand. The locket within his pocket burned with the realization that she'd worn his photograph around her neck. Likely often too. Why?

"I don't see how anyone would want to marry a stranger. We corresponded in a few letters, and he seems like a kind man. But it's not enough for me. I don't feel particularly excited when I think of him."

"Have you ever been excited over the thought of marrying someone?"

Again, she reached for her neck but instead settled on stroking the collar of her bodice.

"Perhaps once."

She said nothing more on the subject, and as much

as he wanted to pry further, he clamped his mouth shut in an attempt to keep himself from asking. It pried itself open anyway.

"What kind of life would you want to have? Would you, as a random example, perhaps enjoy traveling?"

"I'm not sure being Harvey's wife would allow for much traveling unless he took me with him on trips."

"Put Harvey aside for a minute. Pretend you are completely unattached. What would make you happy?"

For the first time since mentioning her fiancé, she smiled. "I would like someplace to call home, but the idea of traveling sounds exciting. As long as it doesn't involve train wrecks and robberies."

"What's life without a little gamble?"

"Perhaps so." Pain rose to her eyes, but still, she smiled. "Two or three children might be nice."

"Children?" He choked. He had not given thought to having children. Ever. But now, he considered the possibility. The word tasted foreign on his tongue, the idea a stranger in his mind.

Another wave of jealousy boiled in his fists. That settled it. Harvey Mason would not be taking Sophia home with him. Samuel could make her happy. He might not be a rich businessman, but he would have enough money after McKinney's bounty to purchase a plot of land. Build a house. Find a way to provide for her.

He ran a hand over his face when he realized far more obstacles lay in his path than he realized. He needed to obtain Sophia's affection, repair their relationship, and seek forgiveness for his lies. Her father's blessing seemed far out of reach. Removing Harvey from the picture would likely prove to be a difficult feat.

Well, shoot.

"Do you want children?" she asked, pulling him out of his troubling thoughts.

Did he? He hadn't even wanted a wife to tie him down. But… "If it's with the right person, then why not?"

The music stopped as the dance ended, and people began lining up for the next set. He held out a hand to her, his heart full of hope. "Dance with me?"

"I only know English dances."

"Then tonight will be an exciting new adventure for you."

He attempted to pull her toward the dance floor, but she dug in her heels. "No. I'm not dancing. I said I'd come to the ceilidh, but I never said I would dance."

"I dare you."

She stopped resisting as she turned to face him, hands on her hips. "Excuse me?"

"I said I dare you to dance with me."

"I don't know the steps."

"They're easy. I'll teach you as we go. You can trust me."

A dubious look passed across her face, twisting his insides into knots. Did she feel as if she couldn't rely on him? She had every right. How could he prove her otherwise?

But then she placed her hand inside his, her expression guarded. "Don't you dare make me look like a fool."

"Never."

He guided her to a group of three other couples, the men facing the women. After showing her where to stand in the line of women, he leaned closer so his lips ever so slightly touched her ear. "This one is called the Haymaker's Jig. It's easy. Just follow my lead."

The music started up to begin the dance, followed by people in the barn clapping along to the beat. Promenade. Jig step. Sophia watched each of his steps intently and attempted to mimic him. Her eyebrows drew together in concentration. She didn't smile.

He was about to change that.

Their turn came for him to take her by the waist and swing her down the line for sixteen beats. A delighted laugh erupted from her mouth as she finally allowed herself to have fun. She smiled during the remainder of the dance, his own heart bursting with joy.

When the dance ended, the audience clapped, and he leaned over her hand to kiss her fingers. "Dance with me again?"

She laughed, her eyes shining brightly. "Just one more."

Between him and Jason as her partners, she ended up dancing the whole night, her smile growing brighter after each dance. After the last dance of the night, her hands still in his, two more roots shot out from his feet and latched tightly to the ground. He wanted this. More than he ever thought he could want something. A life with Sophia. His dear friend. As his wife.

He released a long breath as he gazed into her brown eyes. Two years ago, he could never have foreseen himself wanting this. He would never have faked his death, as selfish as the choice might have been.

Thoughts of her future with Harvey Mason interrupted his happy hopes. She was engaged to another man.

Sophia dropped his hands and tucked a strand of hair behind her ear. "I should go."

"I'll walk you home." *Home.*

"It's not necessary."

"It's absolutely necessary. I need to know you're safe."

She bit her lip with uncertainty but finally nodded. They exited the barn, the tune of a pennywhistle growing fainter with each step into the darkness of night. The moonlight lit their way, accompanied by a chorus of crickets.

She glanced over her shoulder, and he followed her gaze, not toward the barn but in the trees near the structure. The hairs on the back of his neck prickled as he peered into the silhouette of trees. Dark shapes morphed into shadows. The feeling of being watched didn't ease.

He wrapped his arm around Sophia's shoulders and increased their pace, not slowing until the Paces' home entered into view.

The tension in his body relaxed. He didn't need to worry. McKinney wouldn't have dared to show his face around a ceilidh, especially not with him, Jason, and the sheriff on the lookout for his face.

"Samuel?" Sophia said quietly when they reached the porch steps. "You're scaring me. Is something the matter?"

"No. I just want to see you home safe, is all." Dropping his arm from her shoulders pained him, surprising him with the intensity of the feeling. He needed to be near her. Saying goodbye would be difficult. "May I call on you tomorrow?"

A heaviness pressed on his heart as she shook her head. "No, Sam." She climbed the steps but looked over her shoulder at him. "Thank you for a fun night. I'm glad you convinced me to go. When I'm in California, if you're ever headed that way, make sure to stop by. It would be nice to see you."

As he watched her retreating back disappear behind the door, his mouth turned into a deep frown. "Oh, hell no. You're not stepping foot in California."

But he spoke to empty air.

The train would be up and running any day now. He had to convince her to stay with him before it did.

Chapter 8

When it rained in the Wyoming Territory, it *rained*. Bucketfuls of water fell from dark-gray clouds, creating a murky sheet over Wylder. Rain splashed against dirt, forming exorbitant amounts of mud.

Sophia sat on a low stool and stared at the blanket of heavy rain just outside the barn, wondering how she could possibly reach the house intact. Mr. Bailey and his son were helping Julia with a household repair, so she found herself alone.

Her fingers worked clumsily to milk Miss Muffin. A pathetic amount of milk squirted out with each squeeze, attesting to her lack of experience. She hadn't grown up on a farm. She hadn't been bred for hard labor but to be the wife of a wealthy man.

She arched her back against the strain in her shoulders. Her stiff fingers protested against any type of movement in the chilly barn.

Miss Muffin lowed in protest when she squeezed a tad bit too hard.

"I'm trying," she huffed as she swiped a strand of damp hair out of her eyes. "I'm not very good at this." She almost added *yet* to the end of the sentence, but she wouldn't remain in Wylder for much longer.

At the reminder, she touched the tender spot on her temple. Still bruised, but not bleeding. Curse the highwayman who had attacked her and killed her friend. If she ever saw him in the flesh again, she wanted to claw his eyes out. Unfortunately, she wasn't sure she would recognize his face, as she'd seen so little of it. But for as long as she lived, she would never forget the deep drawl of his voice.

She patted the cow and stood, hefting the pail from the ground. Only halfway full.

For a moment, she debated whether to try to get more out or finish her chores quickly to return to the warm, inviting house. In the end, she chose her chores. She could finish milking the cow when her fingers weren't so stiff.

Rain continued to pound against the ground as she stood at the entrance, gauging the distance between the barn and the chicken coop. Only a few yards away. If she hurried, she might not get drenched from head to toe.

Taking a deep, bracing breath, she darted out from the cover of the barn and toward the chicken coop. She attempted to shield the pail with her body to keep rainwater from splashing into it. However, she misjudged the consistency of the ground. Her foot slipped in slick mud, and she wasn't able to catch herself before she landed flat on her back. The milk in the pail spilled all over her. In her hair, her clothing, all over her face.

She spat out mouthfuls of mud, milk, and rain. Tears of frustration pricked at her eyes. An entire wasted half hour of milking! With nothing to show for it.

Anger clawed its way up her spine. She slipped and slid to her feet and released a scream, which the pouring rain immediately drowned. Her anger got the best of her as her foot lashed out at the pail. But the moment her foot left the ground, she cried out as she slipped again, this time landing hard on her side.

A fierce pain erupted in her ribs, awakening the damage the highwayman had done to them. She wanted to scream and cry and shout to the heavens, but instead, she sat in a defeated slump.

She was tired. So very tired.

A pair of strong hands gripped her upper arms and hefted her to her feet. To her horror, she found herself staring back at Samuel's concerned blue eyes. Rain drenched him from head to toe, his hair slick against his forehead and his clothes clinging to his body.

Anger replaced her embarrassment as she stooped to pick up the pail, but when she slipped again, he kept his hand steady on her arm. "What are you doing here?" she shouted over the roaring storm. "I told you not to come."

"Exactly!" he shouted back. "I can't resist doing something someone tells me not to do."

A cheeky grin spread across his face, and she slipped again, not from slippery mud but from her knees going weak. She winced when fire spread across her side again.

His smile fell into a serious look of concern. "You're hurt."

He dragged her through the door of the chicken coop, the small space pressing them too close for comfort. A couple dozen hens clucked on either side of her, each settled in their nests. Rain pounded on the roof overhead, though when Samuel closed the door behind them, the thunderous rain transitioned into a soft patter.

"Did you hurt yourself in the fall?" he asked, his hands hovering but not touching her.

"No." She shook her head as she moved to the farthest corner of the coop to start collecting eggs and placing them carefully into her apron pocket. "It happened when... It happened during the train accident."

Dark tension filled the small space between them. She didn't dare glance his way. Instead, she reached beneath a hen and closed her hand around a brown egg.

"Sophia, look at me."

She shook her head, afraid she might start crying again if she relived those memories.

He grabbed her wrist and pulled her close until she bumped against his chest. "Look at me." She didn't. Softer, he repeated, "Look at me."

Finally, she tipped her head and met his gaze, concern wrapped in the depths of his eyes. Feelings stirred in her heart. An excited flutter stretched her stomach into knots like stringy taffy.

As predicted, tears blurred her vision and dripped from the corners of her eyes.

"Who hurt you?" His thumbs softly brushed her skin. "Mrs. Pace told me she suspects someone beat you."

"Perhaps I deserved it. I hurt him first."

"You absolutely don't deserve it, no matter what you did to him. Tell me what happened."

She attempted to dry her eyes with her sleeve but gave up when the fabric was too wet to accomplish the feat. Samuel reached into his pocket and pulled out a half-damp handkerchief, and she took it gratefully.

"The man who robbed the train. I'm not sure who

he was. He demanded a piece of jewelry from me. I didn't want to give it to him. He kicked me and hit me with his gun. I wish I put up a better fight. He took my necklace anyway."

He placed gentle fingers on her injured side, and despite the pain still throbbing in her ribs, his touch soothed the fire. "I will make him pay for this. I promise you, Sophia. He will be behind bars."

"How? He's probably long gone by now. I saw him ride away." She watched one of the freckles on his face move as he frowned.

"He didn't get away. He's in Wylder."

Surprise jolted through her heart, along with a sliver of fear. "What? How do you know?"

Unease and uncertainty settled on his brow. "Do you know why I faked my death? Why I left?"

The one subject she had intentionally avoided since running into Samuel for the first time in two years raked its claws down her spine. "Don't tell me. My heart can't bear to hear you say you didn't care."

"Is that what you think?" He held her at arm's length, searching her face. "Sophia, I'm a bounty hunter."

Her entire body froze, and now she searched his face for the lie, but she only found sincerity. A bounty hunter? What? How? When? "But I thought you were a ranch hand."

He shook his head, his thumb now making circles on her wrist. "Another lie. One of many, which I'm truly sorry for. Soph, I care. I care so much. I ran into trouble two years ago when a man I had been hunting tracked my father down to send me a message. Yes, my father died in a stagecoach accident. But one caused on purpose."

Shock dripped from her like the frigid drops of water leaking from her clothing and onto the floor. "Your father was murdered?"

His eyes hardened as he nodded. "I faked my death to get him off my trail. I managed to put him behind bars under my alias, Ellis March. I—" His throat bobbed up and down as he swallowed. "I couldn't bear the thought of it being you the next time someone learned of the most important people in my life. Believe me. I wouldn't have faked my death if I thought there was another way to protect you. Leaving you was the hardest thing I've ever done."

"Why?" A moment of bravery fueled her as she held her gaze steady.

"Why? We're friends."

"There has to be more reason. Otherwise"—she jammed her finger in the direction of the exit—"I'm walking out the door."

"Because…because you're my home. I would never have forgiven myself if something bad happened to you."

You're my home. His words punched the air out of her. Her knees wobbled, and she gripped his arms to help her stay upright. What did he mean? Did she remind him of home? Did he want a home with her? Did she make him feel at ease as a home should?

"I don't understand," she finally whispered.

"I think you do. And now that we're on the subject…" He dug into his pocket, and she gasped when he pulled out her locket. "I found this in the coat of the man I've been chasing for months. Care to tell me why my photograph is in your locket?"

Her eyes widened. Her heart pounded so hard she feared he might hear it even over the roar of the storm outside. "Well, I-I-I… It's not what you think." Yes, it was exactly what he thought.

"No?" He moved closer, standing tall above her. "Tell me the truth. Have you been wearing me around your neck for two years?"

She swallowed but stared bravely into his eyes. "Yes."

"Why?"

"I think you know why."

"I want to hear you say it."

Tension crackled between them. Exciting. Nerve-wracking. Life-changing. If she uttered those words, she would either lose him forever or start something she wouldn't be able to stop.

"Because I love you. And when I heard of your death, it shattered my—" Her sentence got cut off as he crashed his lips into hers. She gasped in surprise but quickly melted against him. A rush of heat entered her chest, spreading through her arms and warming her frigid fingers. She tentatively placed her hands on his chest to brace herself as she returned his kiss. A rush of emotions stirred within her heart, from fear to joy to relief.

He threaded his fingers through her wet hair and backed her up against one side of the coop, much to a few clucking protests. She had wanted this for so long, and it was better than she ever imagined it could be.

The heat burned hotter between them as he whispered her name against her lips. Her hands traveled over his shoulders, her fingers brushing against the damp hair at the nape of his neck.

The chicken coop door creaked open to let in a spatter of rain. Sophia pushed Samuel away in time to find a wide-eyed Julia standing at the entrance. The skin around her eyes crinkled as she glanced back and forth between them.

Julia smirked knowingly. "Doing a bit of sparking in the chicken coop, I see."

"No, that's not…" She trailed off, heat flaming in her cheeks as she covered her mouth with her hand—a mouth thoroughly kissed by her childhood friend. She risked a glance at Samuel, only for her cheeks to grow hotter. "Excuse me. I need to…" She struggled to form words when her thoughts and emotions tumbled within her. "Dry off."

She rushed from the coop without a second thought, catching the tail end of their conversation before it became muffled by the storm. Julia said, "Join us for breakfast, Mr. Woods. Can't have you riding out in this weather."

"I'd love to," he answered.

A surge of panic nipped at her heels as she entered the house, dripping wet. What was she supposed to do? How was she supposed to act? What would happen from here?

Too late, she realized only three eggs rested within her apron pocket, and she cursed herself for the shortcoming. However, she wasn't about to go back out there and finish the job. Not with Samuel there.

Heat stole across her face as she deposited the eggs in the kitchen before shutting herself behind her bedroom door. Her heart raced as she leaned against the wall, closed her eyes, and recalled every moment of the kiss.

Home.

What was she supposed to do now? Until the train started up again, she was bound to Wylder, and after...another man. How was it possible to feel unfaithful to a man she had never met? But Samuel. She would cross oceans for him.

She opened her eyes and inhaled a sharp breath as she stared at her reflection in the mirror. "He kissed me looking like *this*?" She gasped in horror, touching the mud caked to her face, the matted hair stiff with milk, the soaking-wet tendrils of hair clinging to her neck.

A bath was in order.

After washing the mud and milk from her hair and scrubbing every part of her body clean, she pulled on a new dress and attempted to pin her wet hair.

The aroma of eggs and fried pork greeted her as she made her way to the kitchen, only to freeze when she spotted Samuel leaning casually against the wall while talking to Julia.

Their conversation hushed, and he quickly unfolded himself from the wall, his eyes wide and full of life. On the table sat several glasses filled with milk, plates, and utensils. She couldn't help but notice the pail on the counter, a quarter of the way filled with fresh milk. She knew exactly who had finished the milking for her.

Her hands on her hips, she stared at Samuel accusingly. "So you know how to milk a cow too? Am I just that bad at it? Look how much I missed!" She waved her hand at the glasses.

"Takes practice." He grinned as he looked at her in the same way he had in the coop—with admiration. "Poor Miss Muffin begged me to ease her of her discomfort."

Julia smiled. "You two take a seat at the table. Breakfast is almost ready. Ivan should be here any minute, but we can start without him."

As she lowered herself in a seat next to Samuel, her pulse thundered in her ears. His knee moved to rest against hers beneath the table. Spurts of ice followed by a raging flow of lava traveled through her veins.

Despite her fluster, she reached deep within herself for a normal sense of calm as she held out her hand. "I would like my locket back."

"Your locket? I believe you gifted it to me."

"And then you rudely gave it back with a letter—need I remind you—informing me of your death. It's mine, Sam. Hand it over."

He dangled the locket by the chain in front of her face. "Itching to wear me around your neck some more?" He laughed when yet another blush dusted her cheeks. "Then how will I get to see your beautiful face every day? I think I will keep it."

When she made a snatch for it, he angled it just out of reach. "Samuel Lyon Woods," she said in as stern of a voice as she could muster. "Now."

"What was the saying? Finders keepers? Help me out, Mrs. Pace. Tell her it's mine."

The older woman chuckled as she set a plate full of food in front of both of them. "Oh, I remember when I was your age. What I wouldn't give to go back to my courting days with Ivan. Such fun times."

Courting. It was a word she never thought she'd ever associate with her and Samuel. But she liked it. A lot.

Another wave of warmth pulsed through her when

Samuel intertwined his fingers with hers and cradled her hand on his lap. This couldn't be real. It was as if she'd found herself in a dream, one she never wanted to wake from.

Just for a few minutes, she wanted to pretend this was real. That it could last.

Then she scowled. "Nice try, Sam. I am not so easily distracted as to forget you still have my locket."

He rested his head in his hand, his elbow on the table as he froze her to the spot with a single look. "There are other distractions I might employ to make you forget."

"Mr. Woods," Julia chided, pointing a wooden spoon in his direction. "You are in polite company." Still, the woman's mouth twitched as if she could hardly contain a grin. "I'm leaving for but a moment to invite the Baileys inside for breakfast." Before she disappeared out the back door, she cast a warning look in Samuel's direction.

The door shut behind her. An uncertain silence loomed in the kitchen, a silence she was desperate to break.

She released his hand, picked up a knife and fork, and said, "I'm not sure what sort of distractions you are implying."

"No? Care for a demonstration?"

Her fork clattered to her plate, promptly followed by a raging blush. Samuel burst into laughter, reminding her of all the times he'd laughed at her expense during their friendship.

She pointed her knife at him and glared. "Is this a joke to you? Are you only teasing me to get a reaction?"

"No, no, no," he murmured. He took the knife from her hand and set it on the table between them before squeezing her fingers. "Well, yes. I do love teasing you. But this isn't a joke to me."

A sudden ache welled in her head, and she pinched the bridge of her nose in an attempt to ward it off. "We're friends, Samuel. Perhaps we shouldn't have…" Her sentence trailed off. She couldn't finish it because she didn't mean it.

"I know. This is strange. And unexpected. But I care for you. More than a friend should."

"Me too," she whispered, still massaging her forehead. "For a long time now."

He grabbed her wrist and pulled her hand away from her face. The blue in his eyes shone more intensely than ever. "Truly?"

"I didn't realize bounty hunters were so oblivious."

"Me neither." A grin spread across his face as he leaned back in his chair. Although he poked at his eggs with his fork, he didn't eat. But then his expression turned serious. "All cards on the table. Right now. Before Mrs. Pace returns." He turned in his chair, his knees resting against hers. "I don't want you to go to California. I want you to stay with me. I know it doesn't look like I have much to offer you, but I can make you happy. We can settle anywhere you want. Laying down roots isn't easy, but I'll do it for you. I'll do anything for you, Sophia."

Squeezing her eyes shut, she took a deep breath and listened to the patter of rain on the rooftop overhead. All her life, she'd yearned to hear those words. So why weren't they enough now?

When she opened her eyes again, she found

sincerity and hope gazing back at her. "Samuel, I... I need stability in my life. Not someone who will walk in and out at his own convenience."

"You know why I left."

"Yes, I do. I understand now, and I'm not angry anymore. But how do I know you won't do it again? If you leave without a single goodbye?"

"I swear I won't."

She clutched her hands to her heart in an attempt to make him understand. "I'm still picking up pieces of the heart you shattered."

"Let me help you." He cradled her face in his hands. "I want to fix what I've done."

She wanted to hope. She truly did. But at what expense?

"I would never have found out you were alive if not for the train accident. What's so different now? Is it because you got caught? Or something else? Tell me the truth."

His gaze looked far away, though his thumbs traced gentle circles on her jaw. "I asked myself the same thing." Finally, he settled his attention on her face. "You are my home, and I don't want another man taking you away. I think it would break my heart."

Releasing a long breath, she held on to his wrists, her hope returning. Could they repair their relationship and mend the broken pieces of the past? Could she rely on him and trust him to keep his word?

"Just give me a chance," he begged.

She nodded, knowing if she didn't at least try, she would break her own heart. "I am short on time, but I will give you as much as I am able." Was it fair to Harvey? Probably not. But she had to know. Otherwise, she feared she would regret it for the rest of her life.

He stole her breath away with another kiss. Sweet and gentle, and nothing like the untamed passion in the coop earlier. Her insides melted. Her stomach fluttered within her, light as a breeze.

"Mmm," he murmured as he broke away. "Even sweeter than your music."

Her shoulders tensed, and she glanced away in discomfort. "I don't play anymore."

"What? Why not?"

"Broken pieces, remember?" She grimaced as she pointed to her heart.

He didn't get a chance to respond as the back door opened. Julia, Mr. Bailey, and his son entered, coats slick with water. Mr. Bailey paused for a moment as he glanced back and forth between them, his smile wide.

"Good morning, Miss Meadows. Mr. Woods. I assume there will be no angry confrontations today?"

Samuel's neck colored. The tips of his ears turned bright red. "No."

"Angry confrontations?" she asked, her eyes wide. "Sam, what did you do?"

"Nothing too awful, I assure you." Mr. Bailey chuckled as he helped Nathan into a chair at the table, one arm still wrapped in a sling. "But I fear for Mr. Mason should you go through with the marriage."

The flush on Samuel's neck darkened to scarlet.

She hid a flicker of a smile behind her napkin. It seemed Mr. Bailey had been right about Samuel's jealousy. This wasn't a joke to him. He truly did care for her more than a friend should.

A piece of her shattered heart found a snug spot to settle within her chest. This could work. Given a little time, they truly could make this work.

The front door opened this time, and Ivan walked in. He shook out his umbrella and left it on the porch before shedding his coat. His wrinkles deepened as he smiled. "Good news for the lot of you. The train is up and running. Just in time too. Not surprising, considering how many people worked on it. The train will depart on Saturday. Tomorrow. To get back on track with its regular schedule."

She and Samuel glanced at each other in alarm. Time was already up.

Chapter 9

Tension loomed heavy in the air. Uncertainty filled each mud puddle from yesterday's storm. Trepidation wormed its way beneath Samuel's gloves and into his fingers as he steered his horse away from town, over dirt roads with sporadic water pockets, and then he veered away from the trail and up an expansive hill.

He kept one arm secure around Sophia's waist while his other hand held tight to the reins. His gun dug into his hip, itching to be drawn at the faintest flicker of danger. Between himself, Jason, the sheriff, and other trusted members of the town, they'd been on the lookout around the clock. No sign of McKinney. But he was convinced the man still hunkered down in Wylder.

"You're pensive this morning." Sophia tipped her head back to look into his eyes. His breath caught at the way her beautiful gaze trapped him so thoroughly.

"I was thinking about McKinney." He glanced over his shoulder, but the roads were quiet. No sign of the remaining two bandits. Unfortunately, the other two behind bars hadn't talked either. "And also about you. I have exactly"—the gray clouds overhead blocked out the sunlight, but he guessed it was around ten o'clock—"three hours to convince you not to go to California. It's not enough time."

"No," she murmured. "It's not."

The horse stepped over sagebrush and waded

through knee-deep green foliage until wildflowers finally came into view. Pink, yellow, and purple flowers cropped up across the hillside, with a beautiful backdrop of the mountains. Sophia inhaled sharply.

"It's beautiful."

Without a word, he helped her down from the horse, untied a blanket from the saddle, and spread it across the ground. He never knew Wylder could be so beautiful. Not until he'd found this spot for Sophia. He wouldn't mind building a house here if only to see her smile each morning when she woke up.

But he feared he was already too late.

He unpacked a couple of pastries and fresh fruit. Nothing too fancy. But he'd rather enjoy the incredible view than worry about a variety of food choices.

"Do you remember the time I convinced you to abandon your chores to take a hike with me?" she asked. She sat on the blanket, her feet neatly tucked beneath her skirt while she picked apart the pastry.

"Convinced? The way I remember it, you threatened to hide poison ivy in my shirt drawer if I didn't accompany you." Although he attempted a scowl, he couldn't help the laughter that escaped as he lay back, his arms beneath his head as he gazed at the sky. "Our parents were furious when we returned."

"It seems to have been the trend. You were a pain in their backsides."

"Me? So says the instigator of nearly every mishap we got into." Warmth bubbled up in his chest as she lay down as well, her head resting on his stomach.

"I was an angel."

He snorted and reached for her hand. Her fingers were cold, so he brought them to his lips to kiss a bit of warmth into them. "Then I must be a saint."

"Saint Samuel?" She rolled onto her side and propped her head in her hand, gazing down at him. "Tell that to the barn cat you shaved. If it hasn't yet died from old age, I'm sure it will still try to scratch your eyes out."

His heart caught in his throat as he relived some of the memories gazing back at him in her eyes. Despite their three-year age difference, she had always been his best friend. The person he'd turned to for anything and everything. He still wanted that teasing and laughter in his life. Humor. Friendship. Love. And he wanted it with Sophia.

"I've been thinking." Soft tendrils of her hair brushed his skin as he smoothed it behind her ear. "This is my last job as a bounty hunter. I might pick up ranching."

"Is this your way of convincing me to stay?"

He picked a purple wildflower and twirled it in front of her face. "Is it working?"

Instead of answering with words, she took the flower from his fingers and tucked it into her hair. Happy warmth encompassed his chest. He'd never understood Jason's desire to settle down with a wife and have children. But now he did. This happiness wasn't something he would find on the road while catching bandits.

Sophia sighed wistfully as she gazed out over the flowers surrounding them. "I wish Amelie was here. Sometimes I feel as if she might appear around the corner at any moment. But she's gone. And she's not coming back."

"No, she's not. But she was so lucky to have a

friend like you, someone who will always remember her."

"And you." She placed her hand on his arm. "Thank you for digging her grave. I'm grateful it was you to lay her to rest."

The memories of those long minutes of grief still haunted him, of shoveling mound after mound out of the ground with the intent of placing someone he cared about inside. When he and several other men had lowered her casket, he'd lost it. He couldn't remember the last time he'd cried, but he hadn't been able to stop his emotions from flowing over after saying goodbye to Amelie.

"Me too," he said in a hoarse voice.

They lay in comfortable silence, watching gray clouds drift past overhead. Patches of blue sky broke through occasionally, only for clouds to quickly cover them up. He imagined children's laughter as they ran around the yard, chasing crickets while he and Sophia sat on the porch swing, cuddled in each other's arms.

He wanted it. Too much.

Several more roots stuck fast to the ground, and he knew he was a goner. If he didn't make Miss Sophia Meadows into Mrs. Sophia Woods, he feared he would never be the same.

"What can I do?" he whispered as he turned onto his side. He trailed a finger over her cheek, along her jaw, and across her bottom lip. "What will it take to make you choose me?"

She closed her eyes and pressed his hand against her cheek. He knew she felt the same as he did. Why wasn't it enough?

"I need to trust you completely. Besides, I feel like

something is missing."

"Missing? What do you mean?"

"I'm not sure."

He dejectedly dropped his hand from her face. He knew the feeling all too well. Something had been missing from his life for two years, and he hadn't known what it was until he saw Sophia again.

Two years.

After a few moments of contemplation, his eyes widened, and he bolted upright. "I know what it is. Come with me."

He grabbed her hand and pulled her to her feet, much to her obvious confusion. When a perplexed frown lingered on her face, he stooped to snatch the blanket from the ground and tossed it over her head. The beautiful sound of her laughter reached his ears as she pulled the blanket off and stumbled after him toward the horse.

If he was right about this, he hoped he would hear her laughter for many more years to come.

****

"What are we doing here?" Sophia asked as Samuel stopped his horse in front of the Five Star Saloon. Many trunks sat outside as if those ready to catch the train dined while they waited for departure. After the train robbery, it was any wonder any of them would dare leave their things unattended.

If they had any valuables left, that was.

"You'll see." He grinned.

He secured the horse's reins to the hitching post and placed a hand on the small of her back as he guided her inside. She blinked several times as her eyes adjusted to the dim light. A group of men sat in the corner of the establishment with a deck of cards stretched between the six of them. Several mothers chased their children around tables and ordered them to behave.

She watched the laughing children wistfully. What type of mother would she be with Harvey in comparison to Samuel? What type of fathers would they be?

A sick dread twisted her stomach at the thought of Harvey and marriage to him. But he was stable and predictable, and his lifestyle familiar. Samuel, on the other hand... Was love enough to sustain them through life's difficult uncertainties?

"Wait here," Samuel murmured in her ear before he slipped away toward the bar. She smiled at the familiar charm on display as he spoke to the older woman behind the counter. He could charm a venomous snake into submission if he wanted to.

When he returned, he grabbed her hand and pulled her toward the opposite side of the room. In the corner lay a couple of empty tables, and behind those—

She dug in her heels, her eyes wide. The sight of a beautiful wooden piano struck a chord of panic in her heart.

"No." She snatched her hand away and shook her head. In two long years, she hadn't so much as touched a piano. "I don't know what you think you're doing, but I refuse, Sam."

"Why not?" He turned to her, defiance in his eyes to match her own. "You used to love to play. You loved it more than anything in the world. I think the reason your heart can't heal is because you won't allow it to."

"Me?" she squeaked, but when several people

glanced in their direction, she lowered her voice. "I have done nothing wrong. You, on the other hand…" She poked his chest to make her point. "My heart is fine the way it is."

"Are you willing to bet on it? Are you willing to throw away what this is"—he gestured between the two of them—"to marry a stranger? You said you loved me."

"I-I-I do."

"Then do this for me. And if you decide I'm still not enough, then I will let you walk away."

The pain within her heart burned fiercely. It hurt so very much, but before the pain could boil over like it often threatened to do, she stamped out the fire and spun away from him. "I c-c-can't. I'm sorry, Sam. I can't let you in. I c-c-can't let you hurt me again."

Not able to face the pain in his expression, she took several steps toward the door but paused as a single, beautiful note stood out in the throng of voices.

A haggard breath escaped her lips as she closed her eyes, the note freezing her feet to the floor. Another note joined the first. The lovely sound pulled on her heart and beckoned her to move toward it.

She remained still.

"Don't," she whispered, but the crowd of voices drowned the word.

Wood creaked as if Samuel sat down at the piano bench. Several more notes followed in a simple song most children knew. Except it was off-key. As if realizing the mistake, he tried again, but the second attempt was also off-key.

The laughter and low hum of voices died down to quiet curiosity. She opened her eyes to find the saloon patrons watching Samuel with expectant stares.

She almost smiled. As far as she still knew, Samuel only knew how to play one song, and from the sound of it, he hadn't played it in a very long time.

At the third off-key attempt, she bit her lip and turned more fully toward his back, hunched over the keys. She couldn't let him keep going like this, no matter how much she desired to flee the place.

"It's a D."

"What is?" he asked.

"The key you're looking for is a D."

He paused for a moment with a look of concentration before he pressed an E. "This one?"

"Lower."

The infuriating man skipped D completely and pressed a B. She would be more annoyed if he was doing this on purpose, but she didn't think he was trying to vex her. How many times had she tried to teach him to play? He couldn't carry a tune to save his life.

"Too low," she said. And when he pressed a C, she breathed out slowly as the man tried her patience. She approached from behind, and reaching over his shoulder, she pressed her finger to the D key.

The note reverberated through her bones and knocked the breath from her lungs. Her head swam with dizzy longing. For music. For a life with Samuel. But teasing the keys was a dangerous game.

"What's the next note?" Samuel asked, breaking her out of her internal battle. "I can't remember."

His calloused fingers brushed over her wrist. The graze encouraged her to touch the keys in a gentle caress before she pressed the next key. The note pounded on her heart, demanding entrance.

She nearly pulled away from the beautiful instrument, but the next note from Samuel drew her in, and she found herself powerless against it. She slid onto the bench next to him, shoulder to shoulder.

"Play me something," he said quietly. "Anything you want."

"I haven't played in a very long time. I can't imagine I'll be anything but rusty." Not to mention the patrons who now looked at *her* expectantly.

"Two years isn't enough time to steal your music from you. Start out slow. Go at your own pace."

The last of her resolve disappeared within the tenderness of his eyes. In a moment of bravery, with Samuel at her side for support, she hovered both hands over the keys. She closed her eyes, and the world around her disappeared. Instead, a fierce wind ripped tendrils of her hair from its pins. Brambles clawed at her skirt. A forest leaped up on all sides of her. An eerie darkness blinded her way.

She played the first few keystrokes and then the next as if two years hadn't passed at all. Her mind recalled every note, every rise and fall in the melody. Her heart remembered, and her fingers followed.

A hauntingly beautiful melody lifted from the instrument, one filled with every inch of her heart. She poured everything into it. Heartache, happiness, disappointment, love, until her entire being bled dry on ivory keys.

Tears fell from her eyes as the sun finally broke through the dark forest, and she found herself in a clearing filled with wildflowers. Home. She was home.

The final note lifted into the air on silver wings,

followed by thunderous applause. She jumped in her seat, forgetting anyone else had been in the room. She hastily wiped tears from her cheeks and found herself gazing at Samuel's smiling eyes. For a moment, she lost herself in his gaze. Her once-shattered heart still lay in pieces inside her, but they solidified into something stronger than before.

"Sophia," Samuel murmured. "I—"

"Sophia Meadows?" someone asked behind them. She leaped to her feet and smoothed down her skirt in her fluster, only to find herself gazing back into a pair of light-green eyes. The man wore a suit, his hat held to his chest. He ran a hand through his blond hair. His strong jaw jumped as he looked her over, and he finally smiled. "I knew it was you the moment I heard the piano. I'm Harvey Mason."

"Harvey?" she whispered. Her voice barely escaped as a croak. The man looked familiar, but she wasn't sure where she'd seen him before.

"Thank goodness you're all right." He pulled her into a crushing embrace. "I departed the moment I heard of the accident. The train headed east was stuck in Rock Springs for days. I very nearly walked the remaining distance. Perhaps I should have." He skimmed his hands down her arms.

A shiver of shock ran down her spine. Harvey had come here? To see to her welfare?

Handsome? Yes. Stable? Yes. But when he touched her, her heart didn't beat for him. It beat for Samuel. What was she supposed to do? What was she supposed to say?

He continued. "The train headed west to California departs in two hours. Are you up for the journey? We can wait to leave Tuesday if you need more time. I know it might not be easy to leave your friend." His eyebrows drew together sympathetically. "I'm so sorry to hear about Miss Amelie."

"Thank you," she murmured.

Samuel butted his way into the conversation and held out a hand, though a flicker of fire lived within his eyes. "Samuel Woods."

Harvey's eyes widened as they shook hands. "The dead man."

"Not so dead after all, it would seem," Samuel replied.

Harvey glanced between the two of them, his fingers drumming against his folded arms as if a nervous habit. But after a moment, a flicker of fire in his own eyes mirrored Samuel's.

"Where are you staying, Sophia?" Harvey asked, a hand on her back as he turned to block Samuel off completely. "We can grab your belongings and board the train. The sooner we reach home, the sooner you will be comfortable."

She glanced over her shoulder to find Samuel glaring at the back of Harvey's head, his fists clenching and unclenching at his sides. She only just found her music again. If Harvey took her away now, she feared it would be lost to her forever.

However, this wasn't a conversation to have in the middle of a crowded saloon.

"I'm staying at the Paces' home. Let's go there."

"I'm coming too," Samuel said.

Harvey's jaw jumped. "Of course."

Chapter 10

Awkward didn't accurately describe the tension in the room, and Sophia wanted to shrink beneath its foreboding gaze. Harvey sat on the sofa, quietly sipping a cup of tea, while Samuel sat in a wooden chair on the opposite side of the coffee table, his tea hardly touched. Julia, bless her heart, attempted to keep a conversation going. It was all Sophia could do to keep from squirming in her seat.

"You will love the view of the ocean from the beach, Sophia." Harvey smiled as he leaned closer. "My home isn't too far from it."

Samuel scowled. *Oh no.*

"And if she likes the view of the mountains more?" he countered.

"She grew up in the city. I'm sure she'll be vastly more comfortable there."

"There's hardly enough adventure in the city. She'll quickly grow bored."

Harvey adjusted the cuffs of his coat. "Adventure means danger. Where I live is a safe place to raise a family. I have servants who will take care of laborious tasks. Sophia, darling, you needn't lift a finger."

Samuel leaped out of his chair, and Harvey followed suit, both glaring daggers at one another. Sophia glanced back and forth between them with wide eyes. Fortunately, no fists had been raised. Yet.

"Laborious tasks?" Samuel growled. "You mean the tasks that give a man's life more meaning? Catching your dinner? Growing your own food? I bet you don't even know how to saddle your own horse."

"I don't need to saddle my own horse to ride one. I could likely ride circles around you, country boy."

The frown deepened on Samuel's face as he took a step closer until their chests almost bumped together. "You wanna bet on that?"

Harvey raised a finger at Samuel, but before words escaped his mouth, Sophia interrupted. "If you two so much as come to blows in Julia's lovely living room, you can be certain I will not find favor with either of you."

Running a hand down his face, Samuel took his sheepish expression to the window and stared out for a long few moments. He rolled his shoulders a couple of times as if to push the tension from his body.

She turned to Harvey next. "I would like to speak to you privately. Outside."

Without turning to see if he followed, she stalked toward the front door and winced when it slammed behind her. Anger fueled each stomp toward the barn. First the incident with Mr. Bailey. Now with Harvey. Samuel should know better.

She paused in her tracks at the mouth of the barn when she noticed a familiar black horse standing behind a cluster of trees. Saddled, with no rider. It swished its tail and pawed anxiously at the ground.

A pounding rhythm entered her heart when she realized exactly where she'd seen it before. In the aftermath of the train wreckage, carrying a vile man on its back.

Too late, she noticed the eerie silence in the trees and the trepidation lingering in the air. A scream escaped her mouth as someone grabbed her around the neck and placed the cold barrel of a gun against her head. Her lungs stuttered with panicked breaths as she attempted to struggle out of the man's grip.

But when he spoke in her ear, her entire body turned to ice. She would never forget his voice for as long as she lived. "Keep strugglin', girl, and you'll find out exactly what this gun can do. You will do everything I say. Understand?"

She nodded past the whimper in her throat, her words buried too deep beneath a pile of fear to dig out.

****

Samuel watched with nervousness in every fiber of his body as Harvey followed Sophia out of the house. He felt so powerless over his own fate, something he'd never experienced before. He'd always made the calls. He'd always known what came next. But now Sophia called the next shot, and he feared he'd just ruined his chances.

"Mr. Mason is a nice young man." Mrs. Pace patted his shoulder. "He likely feels more threatened than you do. Try to go easy on him."

Not an easy task when his fists still boiled with anger.

Tension returned to his shoulders as he watched Sophia stop in her tracks beside the barn. Not to wait for Harvey, who continued toward her, but because something was wrong. His body reacted on instinct as he threw the front door open and drew his gun the moment a man grabbed Sophia around the neck and pressed a revolver to her head.

Fear coursed through his body like a raging current, dragging him beneath angry waters and slamming him against sharp rocks. McKinney stared back at him with a dark expression, though a glint of triumph lived in his eyes.

A tremor raced through Samuel's limbs, yet his hands remained steady on his weapon as he prowled forward like a cat stalking its prey. He reached the spot where Harvey stood frozen but continued toward the threat.

"I would stop advancing if I were you!" McKinney shouted as he walked backward, Sophia stiff as a board. "I haven't shot anything in a good while. You wouldn't want me to start with her."

The man whispered something in Sophia's ear. She shook her head, but when he dug the barrel harder into her head, she complied and climbed onto his horse. He swung his leg over behind her. His gun still pressed against her.

"Please," Samuel begged as he placed his weapon on the ground and held his hands up. "I'll let you go. I won't come after you. Just leave Sophia."

"I'm not sure the men stationed at every exit of this damned town would share the same sentiment. If you come after me, I'll shoot her. If I so much as see your face, I'll shoot her. If you send anyone after us, I'll shoot her."

He kicked his horse's sides, and the creature obeyed. Samuel watched in horror as McKinney rode off and disappeared from sight.

Taking with him the woman he loved.

His chest collapsed, a heavy weight crushing him to his knees. He gasped in a breath of despair and then another until darkness stretched its smoky fingers across the edges of his vision. His stomach churned violently until he thought he might retch. *Sophia.* If he allowed McKinney to take her, he would never see her again.

The reminder urged him to take action, despite the crushing weight on his chest. He swayed dizzily as he climbed to his feet and holstered his gun, then stumbled his way toward his horse.

"Where are you going?" Harvey asked as he gestured in the direction McKinney and Sophia had vanished. "Did you not hear him? If you follow, he will kill her. Let him go. I'm sure he'll abandon her at the next town, and we can retrieve her."

Another wave of dizziness struck as he placed his foot in the stirrup and climbed into the saddle. He closed his eyes and took a deep breath to force away the nausea churning inside him.

He shook his head. "McKinney has done this before. I found the girl's body dumped in a river and a bullet in her head. I can't let him do it again. Not with Sophia."

When he turned his horse around, Harvey stopped him as he called out. "I'm coming with you."

"No. It's dangerous."

"She's *my* fiancée. I'm coming."

The man didn't even have a gun on his person, yet he rode Mr. Pace's horse with finesse. Samuel kept a strong grip on his reins and focused on sucking air into his lungs. He needed to get a grip on himself. Otherwise, Sophia would have no chance of escaping this situation alive.

Jason waved them over at the edge of town, and

judging by the hard look in his eyes, he'd seen McKinney ride past. "He's headed east toward Cheyenne." Jason pointed down the dirt road. "His partner is riding west. They're splitting up."

"We'll go after McKinney. The less people, the better." Despite his trembling insides, his voice held steady. "His partner is yours."

His friend nodded and tipped his hat. "See you when the deed is done."

When Jason rode off, Samuel sucked in another breath as he stared at the long road ahead of them. Too long. "McKinney will likely hold on to her for a day or two before killing her. We'll stay back long enough to let him think he's safe. And when he lowers his guard, we'll make our move."

"How long have you been chasing this man?" Harvey asked, looking him up and down.

"Too long." He kicked his horse forward, eager to do anything but stand still. "Let's get moving."

The sun beat upon them as they started the journey. With so many unknowns adding to the crushing weight of his chest, he knew one thing with certainty—no one was going to make it onto the train headed for California today.

Chapter 11

The wind whipped fiercely at Sophia during the flight out of Wylder. It grabbed her skirt and clawed the pins out of her hair until dark-blonde tendrils flew behind her and, fortunately, whipped McKinney in the face.

He kept a tight grip around her waist to prevent her from falling off the saddle. Eventually, he holstered his gun and slowed his horse to a walk. She focused on breathing, her gaze darting about. No soul existed for miles unless she counted the jackrabbits and squirrels darting past the dirt trail and ducking into trees and shrubs. Nothing stood out. No escapes. No weapons, unless she used a branch on the ground to attack her captor.

Only when the sun began to sink and bathe their surroundings in a golden glow did McKinney veer off from the trail and stop behind a cluster of large boulders.

The moment her feet touched the ground, she stumbled until she caught her balance against a tree, her body sore enough to collapse. Again, she glanced about for a chance to escape.

"There ain't nowhere you can go, girl," McKinney said with a hard look in his eyes. "Don't think about runnin'. You'll sooner die from thirst or exhaustion before you reach the next town."

She glared at him. Instead of mountains of fear and helplessness, anger sharpened its claws within her heart. This man had killed Amelie and many other people too. He was a thief. He'd given Samuel plenty of grief.

And she wanted him to pay for his actions.

She eyed the scratch scars on one of his cheeks and flexed her fingers at the memories. "I like the scars on your face. Where did you get them?"

A deep frown pulled his mouth downward as he advanced on her, backing her into a boulder. He pulled a knife from his boot and pressed the flat end to her cheek. She only continued to glare.

"If you like them so much, why don't I return the favor?" His nose twitched with anger, but instead of injuring her, he pushed her away and tucked the knife into his boot. "We'll stop here for the night. Continue at first light."

He pulled out a waterskin and took large gulps. She eyed the water dripping down his chin, her own mouth parched. But when he caught her looking, he only grinned. "No sense in wastin' water on you. You won't be my hostage for long."

No. Because he planned to kill her.

Nausea churned in her gut. She braced herself against the boulder and took a deep, steadying breath, once again weighing her options. Samuel might not be coming to her rescue, especially after McKinney's threat to shoot her. If she didn't do something, she would die anyway.

She took inventory of the weapons she'd seen on him. Gun. Knife. Whatever else resided in his saddlebags, which would likely be the items he'd stolen from the passengers on the train.

The black horse whinnied and stamped its feet. "Shut it." He tossed a rock at its hooves. The horse spooked at the sudden appearance of the rock and darted a few yards away, but otherwise, it remained close.

So the horse easily spooked. However, she wasn't sure how to work the information in her favor.

But perhaps if she stole the horse in the dead of night, she would be long gone before McKinney found out.

And if he did find out, she'd have to discover just how fast it took to outrun a bullet.

"Thinkin' of runnin', girl?" He chuckled and nodded in the direction of his horse. "I trained her only to carry me and no one else. If you try to ride her, she won't budge."

Drat.

She held her head high and allowed her anger to fuel her courage. "You will have to sleep eventually. Imagine waking up with a venomous snake in your bedroll. Unfortunately, the nearest town is too far for you to survive before you reach a doctor."

A snarl ripped across his face. He grabbed her wrist and yanked her to the ground. She crashed into the dirt and winced when loose rocks scraped her palms.

"Let me make myself very clear." He stood tall, the last of the sun's rays casting his shadow over her. "Try anything, and you will regret it. There are worse ways to die than a bullet to the head."

Despair flickered like a dying hearth within her as she watched him make camp. She feared Samuel might not come for her, and she had little hope of rescuing herself.

But it didn't mean she wouldn't try.

****

Samuel watched the campfire flames flicker, dance, and sway. Long shadows stretched across the small clearing. Reaching, grabbing, clawing. Anxiety churned in his gut. They hadn't reached McKinney in time before dusk fell. A part of him was convinced they'd lost his trail altogether.

He lifted his gaze to the man sitting across the fire, also staring into the flames as he picked at the cooked rabbit Samuel had shot earlier. At this point, he would trade anything for Sophia's life. Even his future with her. All he wanted was for her to live through this ordeal.

Despising the silence filling every gap in the crackle of the fire, he smiled. "I wonder what Sophia is eating. She can't shoot a target to save her life."

Harvey's mouth fell open in disbelief. "How can you joke? Aren't you worried?"

"That woman is capable of handling herself. By now, she's likely got McKinney hogtied to his horse."

Yet, all the same, he stared out over the many miles of road ahead of them, roads covered in darkness. McKinney was a dangerous man. He should never have risked Sophia's life by rekindling their relationship. Her association with him put her in danger.

More silence.

This time, Harvey broke through it. "You know… Mr. Meadows and I spoke at length about you—dead as you were back then—when I asked for her hand. He said he'd been terrified of the day you'd someday ask for Sophia's hand yourself. He was afraid of giving her over to a life of little money. But there was no one else he would rather give her to."

He sat straighter as his eyebrows furrowed together. He'd known Mr. Meadows had been as fond of him as his own son, but to know he would one day ask for Sophia's hand before he even knew it himself? How oblivious was Samuel?

He ran a hand over his mouth, agonizing over his own stupidity. "He really said that? In front of you?"

Glowing red embers drifted into the sky as Harvey nodded. "He needed me to understand just what I was getting myself into by asking for her hand. We talked about her broken heart, how she hadn't been the same since your death. He informed me I needed to be patient and kind in regards to her feelings, and I happily agreed."

The melancholy of defeat pulled on Harvey's expression. Despite them being rivals, he couldn't help but sympathize.

"You talk as if you know her. Sophia said she didn't know who you were. She said she was on her way to marry a stranger."

Harvey released a long breath and smiled wryly. "I must not be very memorable to her, then. We've met several times at social functions. It's difficult to stand out when I was competing with"—he gave him a pointed stare—"somebody else. I thought I could compete with a ghost. I'm not so sure about the living."

Despite his growing anxiety over Sophia's safety, he couldn't help but grin as he poked the fire with a stick. At least he'd won one battle.

Several minutes of silence passed, giving his

growing knot of worry a chance to tighten further. He wanted to kick dirt over the fire and ride out again, but traveling in the dark would do more harm than good.

"I don't feel the same as you do," Harvey murmured finally. "I'm horrified. I'm in a panic. But if I lost her, my soul wouldn't be crushed into oblivion." He sighed, lay back, and pulled his hat over his eyes. "I don't want to be married to an unhappy wife. If—no, *when* we find her, I'm dropping out of the race."

Samuel's heart gave a start as he stared at Harvey. Instead of triumph, his entire being filled with dread. "Don't close the door for her yet."

"Why not?"

"I want her to be happy. And if not with me…"

"I saw how she looked at you after she played the piano. She won't choose me. But she has a place with me if she decides it's what she wants." Harvey said nothing more as he fell asleep on the hard ground, leaving Samuel to his thoughts. Trepidation coursed through his blood. He hoped he wasn't too late to rescue Sophia. If he ended up finding her dumped in a river with a bullet in her head…

He reached into his pocket and pulled out Sophia's locket. When he opened it, he gazed down at her beautiful face. He'd always treasured this locket when it had been his, but he found he treasured it more than ever. He treasured *her* more than ever. When he'd faked his death, he knew it would hurt her, but he never realized the depth of her grief until this moment. He knew his heart would shatter without her in his life.

A tremor entered his hands. His breath shuddered. As if sensing his anxiety, his horse snorted and nudged his arm with his nose. The touch brought him a small amount of comfort.

The fire grew smaller and smaller with each passing minute. His eyes burned from want of sleep, but he knew it would evade him if he even tried. He continued to stare across the dark horizon as he waited for the first light of morning.

It couldn't come soon enough.

Chapter 12

Sophia watched McKinney's sleeping form in the semi-darkness of early morning. He lay on top of his gun, making stealing the weapon a fruitless endeavor— and a dangerous one. She eyed the horse, tempted to find out if it really wouldn't carry her. Another dangerous undertaking.

Her surroundings now slightly more visible, she eyed the ground in search of a branch or rock.

At the thought of smashing it against her captor's head, her stomach churned with queasiness. Red flashed across her memories. Amelie's bleeding head. Another man's bleeding chest. Even if it came down to her life or his, she wasn't sure she could deliver a final, killing blow.

Still, she stepped lightly across the rough terrain and located a rock large enough to fit in the palm of her hand. She slipped it into the pocket sewn into her skirt. Lizards scampered past and darted into a spiky bush. The movement startled a hidden rabbit, which bounded over a cluster of sagebrush and raced away.

A grumble of pain squeezed her stomach. The dry prairie air entered her throat and scorched it from the inside out. If she didn't find a way to escape McKinney's captivity, she feared she would drop from thirst or exhaustion before she even managed to fight back.

For the dozenth time, she stared out over the endless prairie. Nothingness stretched for miles in every direction. But at least now, the path was visible.

She glanced over her shoulder to find McKinney still fast asleep beside the dead fire before she traveled forward. She veered off the beaten path and instead darted from tree to tree, boulder to boulder, in an attempt to hide herself from view. Her gaze jumped from the direction of McKinney to the road ahead. Surely, someone would ride past, or a stagecoach would echo down the path.

Several long minutes passed in silence before thundering hooves headed her way. Her heart leaped with hope, only to squeeze with dread when they came from McKinney's direction.

She darted behind a tree and crouched as low into the brush as possible in an attempt to make herself smaller. Her pulse roared in her ears. Her lungs burned for oxygen, but she hardly dared to breathe.

A black horse and its rider entered into view, setting her heart into a frenzy.

"You think yourself clever, girl?" McKinney called out. "You shoulda thought to cover your tracks."

Dread rolled across her stomach when she spotted the imprints in the dirt. They led straight to her hiding place.

He stopped the horse, threw his leg over the side of the saddle, and landed in the dirt with a *thud* as his heavy boots struck earth. She slipped her hand into her pocket and clutched her rock tightly in her fingers.

"I've been thinking…" he said, each footstep slow and deliberate. "If your sweetheart from your locket comes after us, his first priority will be to find you food and shelter. He won't chase me. I don't need you anymore."

She squeezed her eyes shut. Her hands trembled. And she prayed harder than she had ever prayed before.

But her prayers went unanswered as he continued to move in her direction, slow like a predator who enjoyed torturing his prey.

"Then again." His tone took a dark turn. "I want him to suffer for all the times he's gotten in my way."

Faster than she thought possible, he leaped around the tree, and at the same time, she attempted to slam her rock into the man's skull. He easily caught her wrist, threw her rock aside, and shoved her to the ground. Pain coursed through her ribs as she caught herself against soft dirt.

However, her limbs refused to move fast enough as he drew his revolver and pointed it at her head. This time, he didn't point it at her as a threat but to kill.

I love you, Samuel. Please don't forget me.

His finger moved toward the trigger but stopped as a rattle echoed off to the side. They both slowly turned their heads to find several scaly coils hidden beneath a stretch of rotting log. One of the snakes reared up as it rattled its tail while its tongue flickered in and out of its mouth in warning.

They both remained deadly still, but McKinney's horse didn't share the same sentiment. It whinnied as it backed away from the nest before it spun around to flee. The creature smashed its rear end into McKinney in its flight, knocking him to the ground beside her. His gun flew from his hands.

She scrambled for the weapon. Hope and disbelief shot through her fingertips as she scooped it up and jumped several feet away.

What had Samuel taught her about revolvers?

McKinney froze for a second time when she pulled back the hammer until it clicked. Anger stretched across his face as he eyed the nest of snakes, and then the gun leveled at his head. How many rounds were loaded into the cylinder?

She didn't dare spare a moment to check.

"D-Don't move, or I'll shoot!"

Drat, her trembling words. The only way to make it out of this situation alive was to maintain a level head. She took a deep breath to steady her nerves.

The snake rattled its tail again. A bead of sweat dripped down the side of McKinney's face. When he spoke, he lowered his voice as if to appear less threatening to the snake. Or her. She wasn't sure. "Fine. I will let you live, and you can return to your precious sweetheart. Just give me the gun, and I'll be on my way."

"You expect me to believe that? After everything you've done? You killed my friend in the train wreck. Do you regret it? Even the smallest bit?"

Hardness remained in his eyes as he held out a placating hand to her as he stood. "Of course I do."

He didn't mean it. His words were a lie.

The man lunged suddenly, and she reacted on instinct as she pulled the trigger. The bullet hit the dirt only inches away from his foot. The snakes slithered away in fright. He stopped in his tracks, a scowl on his face.

Well, she'd meant to shoot his leg to prevent him from chasing her, but scaring him also worked. Samuel had always said she was an awful shot. But McKinney didn't know that.

"The next one goes through your skull," she threatened. She motioned with her head toward his horse, who stood trembling across the road. The poor creature. It needed a new home. A kinder home. But after one last favor from her. "Do you have rope?"

"Yes," he growled.

"Go get it."

She continued to aim at his back, and she followed him as he stalked toward his horse. He untied a rope from the saddle and held it out to her, but she shook her head.

"Sit on the ground," she ordered. Anger colored her words, and she wished she had more resources than a rope—and a gun—to make him suffer, or at least to threaten him. He did as instructed. "Now tie it around your ankle."

McKinney's expression soured. "Now hear me, lil' lady. I ain't doin' nothing of the sort. Hand over the weapon, and we'll depart amiably."

His words meant nothing to her. She pretended to inspect the gun. "How many rounds are in here?"

He scowled and finally complied. Enough for him to fear for his life, apparently.

She placed the gun within easy reach inside her pocket as she tied the other end of the rope to the pommel of the saddle, never taking an eye off him. Until placed in a dangerous situation like this, she hadn't realized just how much Samuel had taught her about survival. How to shoot a gun. How to tie a knot. How to make a fire. She'd never thought she'd need to use the knowledge.

Until now.

Gun in hand again, she glared down at McKinney as he glared back. "Should I have your horse drag you back to town by the foot? Or will you come willingly?"

"Last chance, girl. Give me the gun. You'll never see me again."

She raised the weapon in the air, threatening to fire a shot to spook his horse into action. But the pounding of hooves in the distance pulled her attention toward the road. A cloud of dirt picked up behind two riders. And one of them...

A strangled sob escaped her throat as she recognized Samuel's confident posture on top of his horse. He spurred the animal faster upon noticing her, and when he pulled the horse to a stop in an angry cloud of dust, he hopped down, and they ran into each other's arms.

"Samuel." She sobbed into his chest, the gun now in her pocket and McKinney forgotten. She wrapped her arms around his neck and pulled him down for a kiss filled with unadulterated relief. He trembled against her as if his fear melted into immense relief. When they pulled away, his eyes glistened.

"Are you hurt?" When she shook her head, he smoothed down her wild hair and murmured, "I thought we would be too late. But then we saw you with the gun, and we rode as fast as we could."

"Then it's a good thing you've taught me a lot of useful things."

He followed her gaze to McKinney, who still sat sulkily on the ground. "Not quite hogtied." He laughed. "But close enough."

He pressed a lingering kiss to her forehead, and she released a sigh of contentment. The moment he moved to take care of McKinney, she noticed Harvey occupied with patting his horse and murmuring words of encouragement. Her heart dropped to her stomach. Harvey had likely witnessed everything.

"Harvey…" she started. He glanced up at her but otherwise waited for her to speak first. "I'm sorry."

He held up a hand to stop her. "Don't be. I knew the moment I shook hands with Samuel that it was over. You deserve to be happy. I want you to be happy."

"But what about you?"

"Don't worry about me. I'll be just fine."

Her heart surged with gratitude as she smiled. She hadn't expected his kindness nor his understanding. "You will make a wonderful husband to an incredible wife someday."

Although he said nothing, he returned her smile before turning his attention back to the horse.

"Time to take this piece of swine back to Wylder." Samuel motioned with his head to McKinney, whose wrists and ankles were bound together by rope. A gag stretched around the highwayman's frowning mouth.

She glanced worriedly at his black horse. "McKinney said no one but him could ride her."

"Oh, he'll be riding her, all right. Harvey, come help me finish hog-tying him to the saddle."

As the men heaved McKinney onto the horse, a gnawing thirst attacked Sophia's parched throat. She stumbled toward Samuel's mount and dug through his saddlebag until she found a half-full waterskin. A sigh of relief escaped her as she pressed it to her mouth and drank deeply. She left a small amount of water, but it took immense self-control not to consume it all.

McKinney grunted in protest as Samuel roughly

finished tying his hands to the saddle. "That was for kidnapping Sophia and starving her. Believe me, you deserve far worse."

After tying McKinney's horse to his own, Samuel helped Sophia into the saddle and swung up behind her. Warmth pressed against her back as he pulled her close before kicking his horse forward. Harvey led in the front. McKinney grunted and protested against the gag as his horse followed behind.

Clomping hooves against the dirt road filled the silence of dawn just as the sun peeked over the horizon.

"You have no idea how terrified I was," Samuel murmured against her shoulder. "I thought...I thought..."

He trembled against her as if his distress came crashing down after a terrifying event. She knew the feeling all too well. She feared if she set her feet on the ground, her legs might collapse from beneath her.

Exhaustion pressed down on her, and she allowed herself to lean back into the safety of his arms. Comfort. Safety. Home. She wanted Samuel forever.

"You came for me," she said, her voice little more than a raspy whisper. "I thought I might have died out here if I sent McKinney's horse to drag him across the prairie."

"Would you really have done it?"

"I don't know, but the idea tempted me."

His deep chuckle reverberated against her back. He leaned forward, and a shiver raced down her spine when his lips grazed her ear. "I love you, Sophia. More than a friend should."

Heat climbed in her cheeks at his confession. They only grew hotter when he clasped her locket around her neck, trailed his hands down her arms, and intertwined their fingers together, the reins still in his hands.

"Marry me," he murmured.

The heat scorched her, traveling from her fingers to her toes. She turned her head to look at him. No trace of a jest resided in his beautiful blue eyes. But rather, a seriousness and hopeful sincerity gazed back at her.

Despite her fluster, she managed a coy smile. "How romantic," she teased with a playful bump against his shoulder. "My ex-fiancé riding ahead. A highwayman hogtied behind us. I never imagined I would be proposed to on the back of a horse."

He returned her playful teasing with a grin of his own. His smile stole the breath from her lungs. "Makes it more memorable. No?"

"Yes."

He paused for a moment. "Yes, you agree? Or yes to my proposal?"

"Yes, I will marry you." She laughed. "Now stop being an idiot and kiss me."

"Gladly."

His hand cradled her cheek before he dipped down and softly brushed her lips with his. Her heart caught against the sweet gesture. A dam burst inside her, filling her heart with so much joy that the remaining shattered pieces were welded back together and became even stronger than before. She knew she could trust him. With her life. With her future. With her entire heart.

She melted into the kiss—a promise of forever.

Warmth continued to flow through her body as they broke apart and gazed into each other's eyes. She didn't think she'd ever tire of looking into them.

"How are we going to break the news to your father?" he asked suddenly.

She laughed. "I have a feeling he'll be overjoyed. He's always liked you."

"But I'm not wealthy." He fidgeted nervously with the brim of his hat.

"The only thing I've ever needed was you. I don't need anything else." She turned slightly in the saddle, biting her lip. "And perhaps a piano."

Another delightful rumble of laughter escaped his mouth before he kissed her on the cheek. "Now, a piano is something I think I can do."

Epilogue

Laughter echoed across the yard as two children chased the dog and a playful hen over green grass. His little girl's bright-blue eyes brightened when the dog jumped just out of reach. His son more resembled his mother with dark-blond hair and brown eyes.

A contented sigh escaped Samuel as he watched his beautiful children play as pink and golden hues of the sunset caressed the sweet, Wylder air. He tightened his grip around his dear wife's shoulders and pulled her even closer into his side while they rocked lazily back and forth on the porch swing.

Laying down roots had been the best thing to ever happen to him. He'd found a different kind of freedom in his love for his family.

He kissed Sophia on top of her head and murmured, "Are you falling asleep?"

"I'm just so comfortable," she replied, her voice muffled by his shirt. "And happy."

He chuckled and squeezed her shoulder. She repositioned herself to lie back against him while they watched their young children play. After a few minutes, she smiled.

"You are a wonderful father." She turned her head to catch his eye. His breath caught. Even after years of marriage, she still managed to steal the breath from his lungs.

"But I'm not doing anything."

"Just being here is plenty. Your father would be proud."

A happy ache formed at the thought of him and for her kind words. He'd tried his hardest to take care of his family and be absent as little as possible when he needed to leave for Cheyenne a couple of times a year to sell one of his prized bulls.

"Ma! Pa!" Their daughter ran across the yard and jumped onto his lap, followed by his "oof!" Their waddling son followed after. Sophia reached to pick him up.

"You're getting so fast!" he said as he tickled her, and her delighted laughter escaped her. "Soon, I'm not going to be able to keep up."

She breathed heavily, her face red when he stopped tickling her. She handed him a flower and gave one to her mother as well.

"Beautiful!" Sophia exclaimed. "Where did you get them?"

Their little girl pointed to the flower bed beside the house, and he and Sophia exchanged an exasperated look. The things their children got into never ceased to amaze him.

He wrapped his arms around his family and pulled them close. Warmth flickered in his heart as he held the three wonderful people he'd never known he needed. A surge of gratitude filled him. He felt like the luckiest man.

A word about the author…

Sydney Winward is a fantasy and paranormal romance author who dabbles in the occasional historical fiction. She loves building complex worlds filled with magic, strong characters, and emotional stories that can make you laugh and cry.

Sydney is the author of The Bloodborn Series, and when she's not writing, she's reading, thinking about stories, or going on adventures with her children. She lives in Utah with her husband, two amazing kids, and one stubborn fish.

Visit her at:
https://sydneywinward.com/

www.ingramcontent.com/pod-product-compliance
Lightning Source LLC
Chambersburg PA
CBHW072001170626
46813CB00005B/1960